Giosuè

A Possessive Stalker Dark Mafia Billionaire Romance

Calabresi Mafia
Book 6

L.K. Ryan

Introduction

Are you signed up for my newsletter?

Join today and find out all the latest in new releases, contests, giveaways, sneak peeks and more.

www.authorlkryan.com

Calabresi Family

Elio Calabresi - Father, Retired Don
Adelina Calabresi - Mother
Savio Calabresi - Boss
Sante Calabresi - Underboss
Renato Calabresi - Enforcer
Elio III - Consigliere
Vincenzo - CEO of Calabresi Holdings
Giosue': New York Boss
Bosco: New York UnderBoss
Armani: Enforcer

Disclaimer

Warning: There are a few scenes that may trigger. Be aware. Contains strong language and explicit sexual content and is only intended for mature readers. A dark mafia billionaire romance with an asshole alpha male, possessive, and aggressive. This story may contain unconventional situations, language, and sexual encounters that may offend some readers. This book is for mature readers (18+).

Synopsis

Law-school student by day, escort by night – the perfect prey for a billionaire mafia boss.

Penelope has always dreamed of becoming a lawyer, but law school is more expensive than she had anticipated. She has found a way to keep up with her education bills, whilst earning some life experience of her own. Becoming an escort is the most profitable and dangerous thing Penelope has ever done.

Giosuè Calabresi operates by a personal code. Blood, honor, and vengeance are the three words he lives by as a mafia boss. And of course, claiming any woman he desires. For months he has been stalking Penelope, curious about this versatile seductress.

When he finally makes himself known, all bets are off. Will he claim the seductress or will she seduce him instead?

Chapter 1

Giosuè

My knuckles clenched together and I stared as the piece of shit moved in pain on the floor. In spite of Armani's efforts, he disappeared after stealing money from my family. I snatched up my cigar and lighter from my coat pocket, exhaled a cloud of smoke in the air, took another drag, then released the fumes to ease my nerves. I hated getting out of character. As the don and leader, the responsibilities called for me to be diplomatic, calm, and cool, but tonight wasn't like any other night. I had plans to see her, figure out a way to make her mine without causing blood to spill. As a Calabresi, my life had already been planned out and I have only had more stress since stepping into these shoes. One of the reasons I never settled down was that I loathed to complicate my life with the rules and regulations of answering to one person for as long as I live.

I took one more puff, let it ease through my lungs, grinned, and stalked over to the idiot who felt like he could get away with stealing my money. I bent down, pressed the end of the lit cigar to his nose, and listened to the sizzle of the burn.

He screamed, not able to move as my men held down his legs. "Argghhh! Please!"

"Shushhh…You know why I brought you here." I removed the cigar from his nose as the scorching sensation seeped through his skin.

Tears trickled down his cheeks. "I promise to get your money, Giosuè," he pleaded.

"Interesting, didn't my brother set a meeting, and you missed delivering the money, so he had to call me?" I cast the slightest glance to my team, then back up for a minute.

"It was a misunderstanding." Slowly, he cracked open one of his swollen eyes. Blood spilled from his mouth. I shook my head at his ignorance to think I would trust him over my blood. People think I'm a monster and maybe I should be described as one, seeing that I never cared to have empathy or compassion when it concerned my family or business. At thirty-seven, choices needed to be made to further our agenda in the cartel world. Separate from the drugs, guns, and extortion, we ran successful clubs around the city and throughout Italy. Armani, my youngest brother, became the enforcer when he turned twenty-one, and Bosco loved to kill and be in charge like me, so he was the underboss. Guilianna, our baby sister, had moved back to Italy. She was one of our top bosses, managing our business from the borders and ensuring the top political leaders knew our name was not to be touched. Even though Guilianna lived most of her life in New York, I thought it best to have her back in our home country to keep any loyalists from trying to take over. After my cousin, Elio, came to New York, we lined up new business ventures and secured even more locations to spread our enterprise throughout the country. Owning art pieces helped to ship some of our product in and out of the city, plus access to the ports gave us extra eyes and ears from DEA contacts. What Jeremy was trying to pull right now went in one ear and out the other, as though he wasn't in charge of manning the order for a new pill coming into town and securing the money. A shared frown from my closest henchman on Jeremy told me it was time to end the foolishness. I stood, set down the cigar, grabbed my gun, and shot him in both the arm and leg. I moved in closer, staring at his weakened body.

"P-Please," Jeremy whimpered, like a little bitch.

"Only begging you should do is for your family."

His eyes broadened at that comment, as I raised the gun and put a bullet in his forehead. I passed the weapon to Nero. He was my best friend besides my siblings; he was my right-hand man who grew up in the faction and understood his role of being my second eye.

I whipped around to leave, buttoned my jacket, and marched from the warehouse to the waiting car. Nero followed me, then lifted his phone and showed a picture of Jeremy's dead mother, wife, and brother. A clear night view showed the dazzle and glitter of the stars in the sky.

"Where were they found?"

"At some motel outside of Hoboken," Nero answered, climbing in the car and shutting the door. My personal driver started the car, pulling from the dark woods where our cabin was. He cut through the maze of trees and hung a sharp right to get on the main street.

The truck's tires screeched, kicking up gravel on the road. "Burn it down."

A line of streetlights bounced off the backseat. "Already taken care of and the owner is compensated."

"Glad to give them an early retirement." I smiled, lifting a lighter and cigar from the side compartment.

Besides our clubs, warehouses and other business, certain tasks needed to be done outside of the city at remote locations. Buying the property years ago became an investment that extended to owning a lake house in Placid a few miles down the road. To catch a body out here wasn't on my list for today. The two million he snatched up required immediate attention and finding his people before they tried to go to the police needed to get completed. Arriving at Adirondack airport, I climbed out of the car to fly back to the city. Tinsley stood next to my seat on the plane, holding a tray with a glass of dark liquor on it. My mouth watered as I swallowed down the tart smooth taste, and I flicked my hand for a refill.

"Mr. Calabresi, we will arrive in under an hour, and your car is already waiting." Tinsley was a long-time worker for the cartel. She was our trained soldier who took out individuals that wanted to betray the family. Bringing her in was easy as she's a long-time associate with a familiar lifestyle. Her father was my father's banker; he helped him lock in deals when he first got into politics. Not having our parents around and navigating new connections presented me with obstacles I had to try to work through for the siblings.

I opened my fists, examining my knuckles that looked worn out, and removed the seat belt. I hopped up and strolled to the bathroom in the back bedroom. Perched up against the counter, I pressed the faucet on, cleaning up the leftover blood from punching Jeremy in the face. I grabbed a towel and dried my hands. I reached inside my jacket, removed my phone, and logged into the secure camera that I put in place at the hotel. For a few minutes, I scanned each room to see that she wasn't there. My eyes rolled in aggravation. I signed out, moved to my call log, and pressed the number of the one person who knew that I always had to know what was going on, and how much it would upset me if anything changed.

"Boss, before you blow up, I have people on them," Neal explained before I could get a word out of my mouth.

I leaned against the counter, telling myself to count to ten to keep my composure.

"Where are you?"

Neal answered, "Some restaurant in downtown Manhattan."

I grew tense at her being with anyone; on principle, she belonged to me from the moment I saw her, and I'd put around-the-clock surveillance on her until it was time to make her understand who I was.

Her phone records popped up in my email. My brothers laughed at me for being extreme on a woman. "Send me the location."

"Boss, aren't you supposed to handle things at the cabin?"

"The cabin is handled, get the information sent to Nero and make sure the restaurant is aware of my presence." I concluded the conversation, plopped my phone back in my pocket, stomped out of the bathroom, and returned to the front of the plane to take my seat. I scanned the food and snapped my finger for the flight attendant to remove it. Eating was the last thing on my mind. Nero passed me another drink; I dragged it down and bit on my bottom lip. To control my temper was always hard, so the thought of her taking anyone back to the suite pisses me off.

An alert from my phone showed Bosco texting to meet up at the house once we arrive home. Bosco managed a few underground boxing matches where some ended in death. Making money in any type of avenue is the only thing I loved other than my family.

Me: *Back in the city in ten minutes.*
Bosco: *A show happening tonight you should come.*
Me: *How much is the outcome?*
Bosco: *Half a million.*
Me: *Count me out.*
Bosco: *Slacking brother.*
Me: *Have other business worth more.*
Bosco: *Are you going to her?*
Me: *Worry about the money from Jeremy that you recommended.*
Bosco: *Fuck you bro.*

I smirked as the seatbelt sign chimed on as the pilot prepared to descend. I scrolled out of the text thread and tossed the phone into my side pocket, eager to get to my new favorite interest. Me finding love never crossed my mind, since I'm not willing to take on a big responsibility, but there's something about her I find intriguing, mysterious, and set to be conquered.

As I stepped off the private jet and down the stairs, I raised my chin up at the crew. I hopped into our stretch limo to get to Massa Restaurant so I could find her. Anxious as a child who has stumbled onto a new discovery that they didn't understand, I ground my teeth. Memories of the first I saw her hit me. They played on repeat from the encounter from a year ago. The memories made me want to be in her space, knowing her smile could warm the coldness in my heart.

I stood off to the side, arms folded. "Who is that?"

Madam Lucinda sipped her pinot, placing her hand on my chest. "She's one of my girls."

I removed her hand. "You know we've never been like that."

She grimaced, poking her lip out on a sigh. "I very much think it would work out in both our favors if you took me up to the room and made me come." Lucinda smirked with a slide of her tongue across her teeth. Her blatant flirting is more aggressive than usual.

Lucinda, being much older than me at fifty-four, wore a dress with her breasts spilling out and assumed that all men wanted her. Building a life as an escort came naturally to her after seeing her parents start a prostitution ring in New York years ago. They taught her everything about the business. I glared at her, shoved my hands in pockets, and angled to watch the innocent, yet intricate web of lies the girl across the room was creating for her date or client, as Lucinda likes to put things.

"Send her information over to me."

Lucinda squinted her eyes. "Why?"

I frowned and rubbed my chin. "Because I said so."

Lucinda pinched the bottom of her teeth. "She's not your type."

A crowd of women walked past us at the restaurant.

"What's my type?"

"Someone that's obedient, submissive in all ways, able to take your dick in every hole while promising to give their life to Calabresi family," Lucinda recalled from one of the women I used from her business six months ago while caressing my cheek.

I gripped her wrist tight; she tried to jerk away. "My type is what I choose to do with them. Lucinda, If I were you, I'd watch my mouth."

"I understand," she whispered.

"Good, send her information to me and don't make me remind you of what I can do."

* * *

Ever since then I've watched Little Dove, implanting my people at every place she frequents, until I was ready to make my move. While sitting in the car, I read over a few emails, reviewing my calendar of appointments I'd put off until the last minute. I peered out of the windows, watching the streetlights, while the vehicle rolled in and out of traffic. We arrived at my brother's traditional Victorian-era home, the driver moving through the open gates. The house stood on two acres of land less than a mile from mine. We parked and slid out, Nero jogging behind me. The motion-detector lights came on, and the doors opened to his housekeeper, Ms. Yun.

Ms. Yun bowed her head. "Mr. Calabresi."

"Ms. Yun." I walked in, heading to his office, and bypassed half naked women dancing and holding bottles of liquor. Bosco still thought of himself as the young boy our father would take to the strip clubs to become a man. Unless business was needed, he'd be in pussy for the day. Yet somehow, he hasn't had a woman claim him as the father of their child. Not waiting to be called into his office, I walked confidently through the house while the music played heavily through the speakers. I took hold of the knob, twisted, pushed it forward, and strolled inside, not surprised to see a girl bent over with her ass in the air screaming his name.

Her hand pushed back on his chest. "Yes, Bosco!" she screamed.

"What the fuck?!" Bosco shouted, growling at being interrupted.

I raised my palm and pinched my nose. "Get out!" I demanded, waving to the entryway.

She scrambled to move out of his grip and cover up, but he tightened his hands on her waist, pumping faster.

The girl whined again, slapping him on the thigh. "Bosco!"

"Fuck! Suck my dick." Bosco groaned and pulled out of her.

"Not now!" I slammed the door, strolled to his desk, and took a seat.

Bosco finally released her, picked up his pants, and snarled at me. The woman scrambled to put her dress on and ran out of the room. Bosco stuck his hand out for me to take. I glanced down then back up to his mischievous grin.

He held an amused smile. "What?"

"Get yourself together then we can talk."

Bosco shrugged and marched to his bathroom in the rear of his office. Seconds later, the sound of water flowed as he freshened up. Nero chuckled and stood back with his arms crossed over his chest.

Bosco stuck his head out of the bathroom, calling out, "You interrupted my date!"

"That wasn't a date, it was fucking."

"Date, fucking... it's all the same," Bosco remarked, and I clasped my hands together in my lap.

"Where are we with the business?" My patience with my brother's destruction of not caring about anything was pissing me off.

Bosco stepped back into the room and took a seat opposite his desk, lifting a cigarette and lighter. "Jeremy's taken care of, right?"

Our eyes caught; a familiar impatience between us. "Since when do you ask if I've dealt with something?"

"Have to be extra careful."

To avoid having a long evening stuck in a room that still smelled of sex, I growled, "Bosco!"

Bosco hoisted both hands up in surrender. "You need some pussy." Then he reached to flick the lighter in his hand.

Nero chuckled at his statement. I stared at my brother and rubbed my chin. "Answer the question."

"Business is good. The money we received from Jeremy will be put into an untraceable offshore account. I have a few places in mind. Since Vincenzo opened the casino, I think it would be a good time to spread out into bigger avenues."

"Like what exactly?"

"Different areas around the town need cleaning up, and our money could help."

"We already help the city."

Bosco rotated his computer to the side, gesturing to the monitor frozen on the local union website. "Garbage."

"Garbage," I repeated the answer.

"The unions are constantly trying to get themselves heard and were always about money, dropping shipments and expanding. If we get our hands on a few people in the urban areas, we can transport more than enough guns, drugs, and pills to reach outside New York."

I stared at him momentarily. Bosco had ideas all the time, but recently he'd been more focused on taking care of cleaning up any messes. It was surprising to get an idea about extending our billion-dollar business with an untested opportunity.

"What about territories?"

"They wouldn't have a clue because it would be under radar, only us and the union boss."

I listened to what he said, looked at Nero over my shoulder, and waited for him to speak.

"It could work. We would need some people inside to make sure of no interruptions," Nero explained.

"Something goes wrong, then what?"

Bosco's brows knitted in a frown. "Kill the problem."

I grinned, loving the idea of making more money and expanding our name. To keep other bosses from having issues, we might have to take some heads off.

"Send me the exact people, routes, and times that you're thinking of starting. Do you have someone in mind already?"

"Matevi Razin for right now, and we'll see how it runs," Bosco said.

I flicked the lent off my shirt and probed for more information. "Russian."

"Yes, but we can work with him."

"You've made contact?" My brows hiked at the question.

My brother stood, came around his desk, sat on the edge, and logged into a file on his computer. "His background." A business move of exotic animals being shipped in and out of the port docks appeared on the screen.

The idea was interesting all around, and given our name recognition, we could make a bigger dent in the trade business if we pursued that path. Overall work and time meant I needed to hire more people to monitor each route—especially having a contact from the Russian mob making drops.

"I will give him one chance and you know how I handle betrayal."

Bosco raked a hand down his face. "Understood."

"Once again, as the underboss, I expect you to manage yourself with a little more class, Bosco, as my brother or not."

"When did you become our parents?"

"Nero will help monitor the deal until you get more of our people in place."

Bosco pushed off the desk, moved back to plop back down in the chair, and kicked his feet up on his desk. In reply, he blew smoke out of his nose and smirked at me. "Have you seen your girl?"

I once confided to him about Little Dove during one of our family dinners.

"She's not open for conversation."

"Stalking, killing the men she goes out with, and keeping tabs on her friends at school is cause for a discussion."

"Fuck you."

"Brother, the girls are young and in law school. What do you expect?"

I felt a blaze of sudden anger. "I didn't come here to talk about her."

Not caring about anything I said, he shrugged and answered his ringing phone. As I opened the door of his office he called my name.

"Remember she's not one of us. You can't handle her like Tinsley." Bosco grinned.

I clenched my jaw to keep from busting him in the face at that comment. Tinsley meant nothing to me beyond doing her job. Penelope, aka Little Dove, was just a fantasy that intrigued me. Love never came into my thoughts. Nero trailed next to me. We slid in the car and we headed out of the driveway to handle more business.

I was thirty-seven, Bosco was the underboss at thirty, Armani was the enforcer at twenty-eight, and Guilianna was twenty-seven. None of us wanted anything to do with marriage or kids. We loved the life too much to settle down.

I flipped open my grandfather's watch I had inherited from my father and saw that it was already two o'clock.

I had another busy day of meetings and calls with our accountant and lawyers. Once I was dropped at home, I jogged to my bedroom and removed my gun and holster, leaving it on my nightstand. I dumped my shoes by the closet, shifted to the bathroom, and pressed the button to set the temperature in the shower to wash off the day. I climbed into bed, feeling like the moves I had already put into motion might backfire.

Chapter 2

Penelope

I rubbed my arms, feeling the frigid breeze against it. My heartbeat sped up at the change in the wind with her nearness. "Penelope, darling, I have a new client arriving tonight."

I spun around at the eagerness in her voice, chill bumps formed as I peered at Lucinda holding a cigarette in her hand. For an older woman with a terrible attitude who only saw the women under her as competition, she was paid top dollar to keep her delicate face youthful like those girls. On numerous occasions, she'd commented on how I could look like her in thirty years if I earned enough money from doing jobs.

"How many times have I told you I pick the clients, Lucinda?" For the last two years working as a high-priced escort, I'd made a name for myself in large circles by meeting politicians, celebrities, and billionaires who all wanted to lavish me with their money. The goal was to save up enough and leave the business to start my career as a lawyer.

In a small town in Idaho, I was abandoned by my

parents who were young and lacked knowledge. I was mostly raised by my grandmother and rebelled a lot. After she died when I was sixteen, I'd been on my own, trying to survive.

"Penelope, you know I wouldn't put you in a position to not make money." Lucinda grinned, displaying the red lipstick stuck to her teeth, and attempted to pass the cigarette to me. I waved my hand to decline, moving closer to the edge of the rooftop. All my clients met me here at the Walton Hotel before we went out for any social gatherings.

"Lucinda, tonight I have dinner with the upcoming candidate for Congress. Whoever you are trying to connect me with can wait. Send me their file."

Without fail, she dropped the nice smile and smacked her lips. Lucinda knew I would never just accept anything when it was time for a date. Fear had lodged in my mind as I remembered the first time she set up a date with a prominent judge. The guy was too aggressive at dinner, and luckily, I got away by pretending to be sick. Since then, I had done my research on each person before I went out, and I even had security in case one of the individuals got crazy.

"Whatever you're running from, I hope you find it one day." Lucinda rotated, strolling away. Rolling my eyes, I stared down at the cars moving up and down the street. Throughout the past week, I had noticed a long stretch limo parked in the same spot.

"Maybe it's the date Lucinda's tried to set me up on," I muttered, whipping around and walking back into my hotel suite.

Tonight would be an early dinner, and then I could resume studying for the tests I had coming up. I was in my last year of law school, and every day it became a struggle to maintain getting good grades and going out on dates without people trying to have a relationship with me. At twenty-five, I wouldn't let my goals get derailed and trampled over to be someone's side piece. Most of the guys were single, but a handful had wives and tried to act like we could be a real couple. They truly thought that because I was younger, I would fall for anything and allow them to treat me in whatever way.

After I shut and locked the entrance behind me, I looked at my makeup and hair in the mirror, then smiled. Heath was taking me to dinner. We'd be seen in a few photo ops, which I told him would bring more eyes with me being in school. Since he was forty years old, and I was twenty-five, I expected the questions to come at any moment. I grabbed my clutch purse and shawl and headed back out the door. Lucinda always tried to butt into my affairs and handle me, but she was sadly mistaken and needed to divert her attention to the other girls. I pushed the down button and fiddled with my dress, then stepped off the elevator and out of the hotel. It was a largely busy night with people coming in and out, and groups of parties for a weekend in New York. I'd had the same bodyguard with me since I turned nineteen and started working under Lucinda. Devin walked alongside me with a dark mask of arrogance. Many times, I'd told Lucinda he was crazy and attempted to flirt with some of the girls. I knew they'd had sex a few times. She'd done that with a few of the men on her team. Devin's dark eyes glared at me. He moved forward as we got to the hotel's front entrance. Staying in my condo nearby was my only saving grace from the nonsense that came with Lucinda. Devin kept tabs on me and reported back to her whenever I went anywhere, but I ignored them when they tried to pry into my personal business. Heath's wide smile shined on me once I approached. I put on the fakest smile for appearances and let the bullshit from Lucinda flow away.

Heath's fingers hastily drew me in closer. "Tonight should be pretty quick."

Devin put on his phony act, thrusting his hands in his pockets. "Lucinda says thank you for the deposit."

I glanced at him, then glared. Devin trying to handle my clients in my presence pissed me off. Everyone knew I took my cut first then Lucinda got hers, so for him to make that comment meant Lucinda went behind my back and already got the money from Heath. I dismissed my blood boiling at the audacity. I needed to get our plans for the night going.

Heath held my hand, leaned into the side of my face, and pressed a kiss on the rear of my ear. "You look beautiful tonight."

The warmth of his grasp felt different.

"Thank you, Heath."

"I made arrangements for dinner at Lommels. A few important people are meeting to talk about my future." Even though he was a client, I could say he was a very handsome man, but nothing would ever become of us since I knew he had friends like Lucinda.

"Are you sure having me sit in on the conversation is what you want?" I hoped he didn't think I would be some first lady. Heath had tried plenty of times to get me to be his girlfriend, and I always changed the subject.

"Penelope, it's just dinner."

"Simply making sure."

Heath's driver held the passenger handle of the tinted vehicle, helped me in, and shut the door behind me. Devin settled in the front seat, and we pulled off to the restaurant.

"Tell me how your day was."

"Same"

I never got into full on discussions of my life; all he needed to know was if I had food allergies.

He exhaled a deep breath in frustration. "Penelope."

I pivoted sideways to face him. "Look, Heath, we've done this dance before. Just keep it simple and focus on dinner."

He didn't like my response. His phone interrupted us with back-to-back vibrations. He removed it from his pocket and returned the text messages.

Ten minutes later, we arrived at the restaurant and pulled up to check in with the valet when we noticed, a host of reporters were standing outside.

I leaned forward to gaze out the window. "Maybe we should pull around back?" I suggested.

"She's right, too many people here," Devin agreed.

Our driver headed to the back of the building. Heath stepped out, extending his hand for me to take, and I stood close, walking into the old Italian restaurant. Going through the employee area helped us keep the gossip at bay about Heath. Keeping my gaze down, Heath moved us through, giving a few waves to the employees. He was pretty well known in these circles. New York politics came with a lot of money flowing from one hand to another. We made it to the table of his campaign manager, assistant, and a few other people I didn't know.

"I thought it would be a private meeting away from other guests," I muttered.

"Everyone, you remember my girlfriend, Penelope," Heath introduced me, my stomach dropping at the mention of 'girlfriend'. I was halted by an iron grip on my wrist to keep my response respectful.

I gave a curt nod. "Hello."

"Penelope, glad to see you again. Heath has told me

you've been really supportive of him running for Congress," Blake explained.

I held back my glare. "Heath has a lot he hasn't told me about." I placed my clutch on the table, released my breath, and picked up a glass of water to sip. A forced smile would have to get me through the rest dinner, because closed body posture is too noticeable. I scanned all the exits out of habit.

Devin stood near the front entrance of the building to have better eyeline of everything.

Heath placed an arm around my shoulder and pulled me closer. "She's priceless and I hadn't gotten to tell her the good news."

"What good news?"

"I was able to get my name on the ballot for Congress next year," Heath responded.

"As his assistant and you being his girlfriend, it would be great if we got together to discuss his schedule," Jennifer managed to say through stiff lips.

"I'm sorry, that won't be happening," I blurted matter-of-factly.

All eyes looked at me.

Heath's voice was rough with anxiety. "She's pretty occupied with school."

"What are you going to school for?" one of the guys at the end questioned.

"Who are you?"

"Penelope," Heath snapped.

I narrowed my eyes into slits.

"Mr. Nichols is going to be investing in Heath's bid for Congressman. We asked him to dinner to celebrate," Blake chimed in, removing the menu from the table as the waitress took their orders.

"Well, Mr. Nichols, as Heath said earlier, I will be pretty busy with my studies."

Both Blake and Mr. Nichols had a silent conversation with their eyes that could only be interpreted as me being a problem. The only thing I could do was make it known that I would not be running behind Heath—or anyone else. The brief discussion happened throughout the dinner. I let Heath carry on about what he planned on doing once he got into office. I reached for my glass of wine as my phone vibrated in my purse. I picked it up, seeing my best friend, Aspen, checking in on me.

Aspen: How is dinner?
Me: Fine, but boring.
Aspen: Should have had dinner with me and the girls.
Me: I know, but the money is good.
Aspen: Well, I won't hold you up.
Me: Thanks Aspen.
Aspen: Tell Mr. Heath that you're an undecided vote.
Me: Lol!

The crease in Heath's forehead let me know I was making it worse on his team.

"Penelope."

A snarky response was on the tip of my tongue as I glared at him. "Yeah?"

His tone was coolly disapproving. "What's so important it's taking you away from our dinner?"

"Heath." I tried to maintain my curtness.

He tapped his finger on my phone. "We're supposed to be spending time together."

"True, but it feels like the focus is on your career." I

closed out of the text thread and dropped the phone in my purse, then extended my hand for my napkin.

"If something is bothering you..."

"I'm fine." I gulped the rest of my wine and waved my palm in the air to the waitress for a refill.

"You've had enough," Heath whispered harshly.

A flicker of irritation surged through me. "Heath, if you continue trying to be my father our dinner will end."

"Heath, maybe we should table the discussion for another time. Like she says, we can talk business on a later day," Blake said.

I wasn't sure what had gotten into Heath tonight, Normally we had a good time, but I guess he felt some type of way and wanted to exert some power.

I stood from the chair and grabbed my purse. "Actually, I'm feeling a little under the weather. I am going to head home."

Heath stretched his hand to grasp mine. "Penelope, we had plans."

"Heath, obviously she's not doing well. Let the lady return to her place." Jennifer, his assistant, frowned at me.

Devin stalked over as I yanked my grasp out of Heath's hold. "She's right. We can catch up another time." I bent down and kissed him on the cheek to ease the tension, sauntered from the restaurant to the limo, and climbed in, kicking off my shoes and rubbing my temples to work out the headache that was building. Lucinda would probably be pissed that I left early and would want some of the money back to make up for Heath not getting his full date. At the moment I had a good enough amount in my savings to reimburse him partially, but I knew Heath desired more and that was something I would never be able to give him. Men like him wanted to make it seem like I was some helpless damsel in distress who needed assistance. There's nothing in this world I would need saving from that would make me call Heath. Lucinda came into my life when I had no one, but at nineteen, I knew her real intentions, and I wasn't gullible to her charms.

After swerving in and out of traffic, we got to my condo, and I stopped the driver at the curb and told him that I would be in touch. Devin tried to hop out, but I blocked him.

"Lucinda wants you to call her." Devin held up his phone with Lucinda's name scrolled across the screen.

"I will when I'm ready." I strolled into my building, feeling the long day drain from my body. I turned the knob after slipping the key in and flicked on the lights to my safe space. The memories of living from shelter to shelter, carrying around the same bag of clothes, some nights not sleeping to make sure I still had that same bag in the morning. Then foster homes weren't better, some people would just ignore you and running away to sleep in parks and motels. It caused me to be more cautious of people. I became even more dependent on myself and never letting anyone get close to hurt me again. The disappointment I felt as a child while foster parents only cared about the money they'd get and leave me without food, clothes on many nights. Now, I could have my own place without anyone trying to take it away or force me to be something that I wasn't. I tossed my shawl and purse on the side table and came out of my heels, letting my hair loose. The red gown peeled right off my body. I was only wearing a thong underneath. I hung the dress up against the bedroom door to get it cleaned. At my 5'9" height, with my thick thighs, round ass, and full breasts, I was glad to not be the ideal size that people tried to pressure women into being. My tired green eyes stared back at me through the mirror in the bathroom. I sighed, prepared to shower and study for the rest of the night. I turned on the faucet, cleaning my face and letting the tub cool down before I climbed in and soaked.

I finished bathing, made a sandwich to eat with chips, and laid my books on the bed. Feeling more relaxed, I flicked on the TV trying to search for a program to watch but paused on the news station.

"We have candidate Heath Arnold coming out of this famed restaurant, with his entourage beside him," the newscaster explained. I muted the channel and watched Heath wave at a few people and jump in a blacked-out SUV.

"Pathetic." I took a deep breath, then gazed down at my papers on my bed.

I marked a few more chapters in my notebook and fell back onto the pillow, rubbing my tired eyes as they fluttered. Slowly a heavy sleep came upon me.

* * *

I opened my eyes, feeling exhausted from the previous day's events. I slid out of bed, then walked to the bathroom to brush my teeth and get ready for the day. I had a study session planned for later, then I would be hanging with Aspen for a girls' outing. I checked the time. It was going on 9 AM, and my first class was at 9:45, so I had a small window to eat breakfast. Once I had my purse, backpack, and phone I headed out.

"Penelope, something came for you." The security guard gestured to me at the front desk. He pushed over some flowers. "Someone's interested." Mark winked at me.

"Is there a card?"

He held the sign-out sheet for me to check off that I received the gift.

"No card this time."

"Thanks, Mark. Do you mind leaving it at my door?"

"Sure, as long as I have your permission."

"You're amazing Mark, thank you." I grinned, placing a twenty-dollar tip on the counter for him.

I lifted my phone to answer as I came of my building. "Hello, Lucinda." The sun shined bright, and there was a light wind. Glad I wore a thinner sweater above my shirt.

"You have cost me money, little girl." Her mood veered into anger from our last conversation.

I spoke with a hint of bitterness. "Lucinda, calm down."

"I hope you know that means you'll have to pick up extra dates this week," she snipped.

Being that it was Thursday and then this weekend I had plans to relax, Lucinda needed a few reminders of what I would and wouldn't do.

"My personal time is booked."

"No, you have me fucked up!" she shouted.

I paused, waiting for traffic to go by, and crossed the street as horns blew. Lucinda continued to argue over the phone. I waited for the light to turn and walked a few blocks to the subway.

"The money will be in your account in a few minutes."

I heard bitterness spill into her voice. "Heath is not only an important client, but my name is also on the line if you continue to drop the ball."

I shifted my weight. "Okay, Lucinda."

"Glad you're listening for once."

"Do you have Devin following me?" I glanced at the blacked-out limo that I had noticed from my building approaching the same light that I crossed.

"No, why?"

I bit my top lip. "Nothing." I shook off the thought. Maybe Heath sent someone.

I pushed through the crowd and headed downstairs, hanging up on Lucinda and paying for the ticket to hop on the train. Going to Columbia University and living alone in New York made every decision to keep certain things under wraps even more important for me.

As soon as I took a seat, the train was loaded up with more passengers. I gazed at all the individuals going about their day, having no clue about each other's lives.

Not long after boarding we reached my stop. I climbed the stairs, passing a few students that were headed into the building. I froze at the sight of the same sleek vehicle parked at the corner near the library.

I muttered to myself, "Lucinda's men probably."

I shrugged it off and ambled inside to grab something to eat from the dining hall before class. Today was going to be packed with catching up on my studying and talking with my professors on any extra credit I could do. I'd do any and everything to have my resume look good for graduation and finding a job.

I strolled out of the building hours later and felt eyes on me. I scanned the area, not seeing the car in the spot from before.

"Penelope!"

I continued walking, ignoring my name being called by the asshole I gave my heart to when I first got here. A tug on my arm caused me to stop, look down, then glare up at Alden grinning in response.

"Alden, let me go." That smile would have had me blushing years ago, but now it only made me sick to my stomach. We'd dated in the beginning of my first year there, and everything had started out fine—until he became more popular. That led to a big ego and girls wanting to know him.

Those dreamy eyes I fell for flickered in my direction. "Come on, haven't you missed me?"

I jerked my arm away. "Actually, I haven't."

Alden surveyed me with his eyes. "I'm having a party at my place."

"Not interested."

Aspen had warned me about dating him, and at first, I looked the other way, not wanting to let in the charm and influence of someone I thought really cared about me. He knew about me being abandoned and losing my grandmother, and he'd used that to lie and cheat on me, thinking I would always stay and forgive him. Many phone calls went unanswered when I tried to get in touch with him, and one particular night I had planned a surprise dinner for his birthday and explained to him about meeting at his place for a study session. Well, to my surprise, I came too early that night and found him in bed with another woman. The same woman he was caught making out with at a party after we'd been together for six months.

He constantly called and brought me gifts until I finally heard him out one day. He apologized and promised it was a situation that meant nothing.

"Baby you know I still love you." Those large brown eyes peered at me.

"I have to go."

"Penelope!" I whipped around to see Aspen waving from her car. I ran over and hopped in, tossing my bag in the back of the vehicle.

Lucy, my other close friend, sat up from the backseat. "What was he talking about?"

I sighed. "Same story about wanting me back."

"Funny, because we saw him in Elisha's face an hour ago." Lucy whistled, then sipped a drink.

Knots coiled in my belly. "He's crazy if he thinks I would want him back."

My group of friends knew my life outside of school and supported me even if they didn't agree with the escort lifestyle. Aspen worked for her family's business, which was a catering company, and she went to school at Juilliard. Lucy went to Columbia with me and wanted to be an entertainment lawyer. All three of us planned to take a vacation after graduation as a gift to ourselves. Lucy's family had more money than the two of us combined, but she always stayed humble and I appreciated her when I was down on my luck and needed help.

Aspen's long blonde hair flew through the wind, her red nails tapped on the steering wheel as we listened to Jessie J. While she drove, I took out my phone to see if my bank delivered the money to Lucinda to get her off my back.

Aspen probed. "How was your date last night? Did Lucinda send Devin again?"

"It was fine. Heath tried to make it more than it was again." I made a note for myself to end all future communication with Heath. "Hopefully, he gets the idea because I plan on putting him on the blocked list. I saw on the news last night a few pictures with me in them from the side profile."

Lucy pressed the radio button. "He's running for Congress. Dating him would only put a bigger target on your back."

"Exactly, he thinks I will change my mind about us dating and being public."

"Men are always trying to pin us single ladies down."

Lucy held her phone up and fluffed her brown curls to snap a few selfies. She and I were the only ones' single. Aspen had been in a relationship for the past two years with a guy named Stewart. He was pretty close to the ideal boyfriend and I loved how much he cared for our friend.

Wind blew in my face, and I tapped my hand on my thigh to the beat of the music. "Where are we going for lunch?"

"I want a burger and fries." Aspen turned off on West 21st Street.

"That's fine."

Lucy leaned forward, showing us a picture of a dress on her phone. "This weekend is set for the party. We need to find something to wear."

I sat back, adjusted the seat, and pondered of how to handle Lucinda's demands, school, and Heath's possessiveness.

Aspen nudged me in the shoulder. "Hey, you're too quiet." She gunned it into overdrive to get to the restaurant.

"Just thinking."

Aspen put on the left turn signal. "About what?"

"Feels off, like something's different."

"Duh, you're about to graduate." Lucy pinched me on the arm.

"Well, I still have a few more months—at least six—before I obtain my degree. The few internships I applied for haven't responded."

My dream was to be a family attorney and help save future kids from the same things I went through as a child. My parents had dumped me on someone else's doorstep, and I never heard from them again, only to uncover years later that they were dead, and we could never have a relationship. Sometimes I wanted to stay in a hate-filled state, but I knew that keeping my emotions in that space would never work.

Aspen parked at Spark Burger Café down from the school. She turned off the car and climbed out of the driver's side. Lucy playfully slammed me on the butt. We linked our arms together and headed in to eat and relax, while Aspen told us about the party that would be happening this weekend.

Chapter 3

Giosuè

I laid the cigar in the ashtray while watching her on the camera footage from Lommels. This morning, I watched her on campus. A bunch of flowers were delivered to her condo early, but I left the card off. I wanted to see if she would accept them. A few of my soldiers told me she'd seemed to notice them around, so they stayed back a little farther to not rattle her. Bosco was probably right that I should leave her alone—she was young, and getting involved with someone like me would put her life in danger —but I couldn't keep my mind from racing whenever I saw her face. I sat back and stared at pictures of her with a few men at different events. Then I went over to the footage of her leaving the restaurant with her guard. I replayed the video from the other night at the hotel of her walking through the lobby with a fake smile on her face to greet Heath Laurier. The bastard had no idea who she belonged to and I clenched my fist in aggravation at how he was holding her around her waist like they were a real couple.

"What's the point of inviting me here?" Tinsley stood near the bedroom wearing only a robe and skimpy lingerie.

Our relationship was strictly business but she felt like I should give her more.

I had a meeting scheduled in an hour and needed to let off some stress. She came in with a wide smile and tried to kiss me on the lips, but I turned my face away.

"We have a meeting."

Tinsley brushed a hand down my chest. "Then I could have met you there." Heat radiated from her.

I turned my head and gazed into her crystal blue eyes. "Come here."

Tinsley slowly lifted the robe from her shoulder, dropping it on the ground and standing between my legs.

"Get on your knees and open your mouth. Maybe putting something in there to keep you busy will shut you up."

She rolled her eyes and reached for my belt buckle. I grasped her wrist. "If it's a problem, you can go."

A flush of embarrassment rose on her cheeks. "No problem, Giosuè."

I drew air in my nose. "What did you call me?"

"Giou... I mean, boss." Tinsley lowered her head, slowly stroking my dick, and swiped her tongue around the tip.

I dropped my head back on the couch. I inhaled a breath, flicking through pictures of Penelope at her condo, at school, and hanging out with her friends.

Tears stung her eyes. "Mmmmmm... Giosuè."

I grunted and cupped the back of her head. Tinsley had started to go faster and faster, when banging on the door interrupted us.

"Come in!" The constant thoughts of her in my mind worried me. Whatever this new feeling was needed to go away.

Tinsley tried to stop and get up.

I tightened my hand around her neck. "Keep going."

"Giosuè!"

I groaned, pushed her face down farther into my lap to get my nut, and pumped faster into her mouth until I felt a tingle in my spine.

"Keep—Sh—" I groaned.

The door cocked open. "G, they're ready." Nero slipped through the door. I logged out of the file and tapped Tinsley on the shoulder.

Nero swiveled around to give me his back.

It seemed like forever since I'd had her in this position— only if she knew it was because of another woman. "Here I come," I replied.

Nero chuckled and shut the door behind him.

"Get up."

Tinsley paused then removed my dick from her mouth. "But I wasn't finished."

"We have business to handle. Wash up and look presentable."

Tinsley stood, ran a hand across her chin to get the excess cum off her cheek, and turned to go into the bathroom. "Are we going to finish later?" Her eyes held hopefulness.

"That was the last time, Tinsley."

She swished her hips, held a warm towel in her hand, and wiped my dick clean. "Yes, sir."

Her interest would end once she had another job to do.

I caught up with Nero, and we sat in the back of my bulletproof vehicle on our way to meet up with Bosco and his contact who handled the trash pickups. Saturdays weren't reserved for business, and I mostly enjoyed spending time at my lake house in upstate New York. The only people who were aware of my secluded palace were my brothers, my cousins, and my best friend. I liked to lock myself away from all the noise. Riding horses, sitting in my boat, and blowing off some steam with my guns were the perfect ending after a long week.

"Bosco said they've checked him for weapons and wiring."

Going back in time I might have had a different life outside of killing and running the cartel if my parents hadn't been one of the legacy names. "Good."

"We're here." Nero chucked his chin up as the car stopped at the back of the local club that's on average closed during the afternoon, unless there was a special event. It was in a prime space, near college campuses and shops. I held up my hand for Banner to stay in the car. Nero jumped out, followed by Tinsley, and then me.

"You ready?" Nero glanced at Tinsley to let her know to put all emotions to the side and do her job if needed.

"Always ready to protect the Calabresi name." Tinsley clasped her hands together and stalked off wearing a black catsuit underneath a trench coat with her gun secured.

Nero stood in the back, me in the middle with my other men securing the sides, and the rest on top of the building across the street.

Today it wasn't raining, but I could feel a coldness brewing. Something was bound to happen today if anyone felt like shedding blood after years of watching my cousins face danger. I liked to be prepared to take out anyone who tried to hurt my family.

The music was off and a few workers walked past not saying a word. I kept my eyes ahead after checking out the exit points. In the back corner, a few women sat giggling together and waved at me. I ignored the gesture and continued to the back of the club, following Nero through the corridor into the employee break room.

"Gentleman." I scanned the four men sitting around talking. Bosco and Armani stood to shake hands with first me, then Nero. Matevi sat up straight with his hands firmly on the table. His eyes held contact with mine, letting me know that he wasn't intimated by the amount of people surrounding him.

I pulled out the chair and sat down before him. "Matevi."

Tinsley stood on my right, Nero to my left, and my brothers focused on the guest before us, all eyes watching with interest.

Matevi spoke. "Giosuè."

The light on the ceiling suddenly flickered. "My brother tells me you want to do business." I pointed at Bosco.

Matevi sat back with his arms folded over his chest. "True, we have a lot in common." His beige suede sports-coat stretched.

"What would that be?"

He reached into his pocket and slowly removed a match. "Wealth beyond our imagination." He smirked, flicking the light in his hand.

"Something like that, but as you know I never do business with just anyone. How concerned should I be if you double cross us?"

"I have no plans on losing out on money. Me being here is a sign that I run on my own without a boss."

My distrust caused him to pause and narrow his brow in reservation.

"No ties to the Russian mob or anyone else?"

Matevi chuckled. "I didn't say that."

"I called you, Matevi, because you drive on the route that goes through downtown Manhattan. That could be very big for us—and a hazard if we get caught," Bosco reminded him.

"We should start in smaller sections," Armani chimed in, checking the time on his watch.

I swept my eyes over to him. "Are we keeping you from something?"

Armani frowned and rubbed his chin. "I have work, and the last-minute meeting pushed it back." He gave an impatient shrug.

"Matevi, do you have little brothers?"

Matevi's fingers brushed across his chest as he replied, "No."

"Lucky you." I laughed and Armani glared at me.

Bosco cleared his throat, reached into his pocket, and removed his cell. "We want to have our product going to each individual district. Can you make that happen?"

Matevi's hand came down to pick up the phone and he stared at the pictures. "How much are we talking?"

I replied, "Ten percent."

"Twenty," Matevi challenged.

"Ten—and if we have no issues for the first six months, then we'll revisit the percentage."

Matevi flung his hands up. "I am taking all the risks."

"You are—and my brother explained that you could handle the risks. I mean, you want to be rich, correct?"

Matevi's gaze went from me to Tinsley. "Who is she?"

"No one that concerns you."

Matevi pushed his lips together and blew her a kiss. "Is she going to be doing the pickup?"

I wasn't above using every resource to get what I want. "Will that make things easier for you?"

Tinsley gasped. My head turned toward her in a glare. Matevi licked his lips. "Are you selling her to me?"

"I'm not for sale." Tinsley gritted her teeth.

"We have other women for that. Tinsley is my eyes and ears on the ground and in the air."

"What about the animals?"

"Animals?"

"We need to use your docks, and we will cut you in on a finder's fee twice a month. About five million."

Bosco leaned forward, pointed at him. "Just to use our docks, you have your own security."

Matevi arched one black brow. "Yes, but we need the paperwork to look right. I understand you import and export art."

"I do, one of my passions."

Matevi stuck his hand out for me to take. "Then we can do business, Mr. Giosuè Calabresi."

I extended my hand to grip his, forcefully tugged him forward over the table, and quirked an eyebrow. "The second I suspect you've fucked me and my brothers over, Tinsley will cut your dick off and feed it to your mother as she burns alive. Do I make myself clear?"

Matevi looked at Bosco, then at Tinsley, biting his lip. "Clear."

"Great. Armani, make sure you have Matevi taken care of with the location for the ports—and Bosco, get the product packed up."

I rose from the chair and turned to leave with Nero and Tinsley trailing behind. When my phone dinged in my pocket, I removed it to check the message.

Giosuè

> **Macsen:** *She's on the move.*
> **Me**: *Where?*
> **Macsen:** *At the mansion.*
> **Me**: *And Lucinda?*
> **Macsen:** *She just arrived there.*
> **Me:** *On my way out.*

I told Lucinda that I didn't want Penelope anywhere near the mansion—it was bad enough that she had the hotel as a pickup location. Macsen sat in the passenger seat monitoring video, while Banner had the car running. Tinsley held a harsh expression I had no time to investigate. I looked at her intently, then strode to the backseat.

Tinsley stepped close to me as I held the door open. "Giosuè, we need to talk."

"Nero make sure she gets all the information of where to be for the drop off points."

"Giosuè." Tinsley shifted indignantly from foot to foot.

"Tinsley, either you want you keep your position or you don't. I have other things to handle and you are the last of my problems."

Nero typed away on his cell phone, and I picked up mine, noticing a text from him.

> **Nero:** *She's in love with you.*

His mouth moved into a smile.

> **Me:** *She would be wise to focus on her job.*
> **Nero:** *Where are we headed?*

Me: *Macsen spotted Penelope at Lucinda's mansion.*
Nero: *You going in guns blazing?*
Me: *If she's fucking someone, yes.*
Nero: *And Tinsley?*
Me: *What about her?*

Nero slouched against the seat.

Nero: *You don't think taking your plaything to meet your future wife would be a little rude?*
Me: *I'm not marrying Penelope and Tinsley knows we only hook up.*
Nero: *I warned you.*

I ignored his gripes and logged into the security cameras I'd had placed at Lucinda's when I first found out about Penelope and decided to research Lucinda's business more.

* * *

The gated mansion looked like a place where a family could live. There were acres of grass and a gold-plated iron gate with a large "L" in the middle. I hadn't planned on making myself known but hearing that she'd come here—and not the hotel, or her condo—had me on high alert.

I jumped out of the car and stalked inside without waiting to be announced. Nero, Tinsley, and Macsen tried to catch up. I marched to her office, not knocking, and forced my way in. I paused at what I barged in on. Lucinda was bent over her desk, and Devin had his pants around his ankles.

"Giosuè!"

A vein throbbed. "Where is she?"

Lucinda shoved Devin backwards and pulled down her dress. "Where is who?" Lucinda combed a hand through her hair, slipped her feet into her heels, and plopped down into her chair.

"Penelope."

"Why are you looking for Penelope?" Devin questioned.

"I got word she was here, Lucinda." I ignored his question.

Lucinda gave a breathless laugh, picked up her cigarette and lighter. "She came by about ten minutes ago but left."

I scanned over her, trying to find any inkling of a lie. "Lucinda, my patience is very thin."

She smiled, puckered her lips, and blew smoke from her cigarette. "Giosuè, you need to understand that I run a business."

"Fuck your business." What Lucinda didn't know was that I had a lot of control and a competent way of handling myself. Her business was in the process of going away, and soon she'd learn I was not to be played or lied to.

Devin stepped in front of her desk to block my line of sight.

"Devin, it's okay," Lucinda muttered, then stood and came around her desk.

I craned my head to the left. "Tinsley."

Tinsley took a step forward, removed her gun, and held it to the side of Devin's head. Lucinda tried to reach for Devin's hand.

"Lucinda, tell your little boytoy I will kill him next time he gets involved in my business."

Lucinda pinched her lower lip and whispered, "Yes, Mr. Calabresi."

"Good, and another thing. Penelope is no longer going to be available for Heath Laurier—or any other clients."

Her eyes fell into slits. "I understand."

"Glad we have an understanding."

I snapped my fingers and Tinsley withdrew her gun. Devin relaxed through breaths, watching us walk out of the office. The three of us jumped back in the car to leave.

"Who is Penelope, Giosuè?" Tinsley probed. Her features twisted in a maddening leer.

"No one you should worry about."

She huffed, folded her arms, and sat back. Banner pulled out of the driveway, taking off towards my office.

"Nero send flowers to her condo."

"Flowers?!" Nero and Tinsley yelled in unison.

I tapped on my phone and dialed my brother's number. It rang twice before his voice message came on. I hung up and tried again. Finally, he picked up after the third ring.

"I'm busy," Armani said as loud screams came through the phone.

A cynical smile played on my lips. "Should I be worried?"

Armani responded, "No."

"I should be at the office in a few minutes."

Armani cleared his throat. "Matevi has the locations."

"Banner, drop Tinsley at home," I explained, lifting my wristwatch to check the time.

Tinsley grasped my arm, and I pushed her away. "Giosuè, I want to finish having our conversation." That woman's natural state was to figure out how to make something more than it really was.

"After you finish, I need another job done."

"What?" Armani wondered.

"Come to the office, not over the phone."

Armani hung up without answering me, and I smiled at his annoyance. The next call that I placed got picked up right away, loud music blasting in the background.

"Bosco."

"Yeah!"

"It's time."

Bosco said, "On it now."

We made it to the main offices of Calabresi Corporate that we'd built, where we handled all our distribution from import and export, and legal and illegal money that I had funneling through multiple business from nightclubs, art galleries, and investments. Macsen, Banner, and rest of team departed the cars alongside me and made it inside the building. My brothers stood around the conference table. Nero was to my right with two of our best shooters. All wore attentive expressions, waiting on my word.

"As the Underboss, I have to make sure to question if a kidnapping makes sense," Bosco remarked, leaning his knuckles on the table.

"Lucinda's getting out of hand."

"Is this about Lucinda or your obsession with Penelope?" Armani inquired, adjusting the cold steel gun on the table.

I twisted to the right to see the arched brow from my little brother. "Both. I need Lucinda shut down and Heath silenced."

"Going after a congressman will make things more complicated," Armani explained.

Bosco raised a hand to scratch his chin. "Armani's right. I've been down with you about Penelope, but now the deal with Matevi could be compromised if we take out his biggest client."

"What do you mean?"

Bosco and Armani made eye contact. They often kept secrets from me or tried to handle something before I became aware.

"I found out that Heath and Matevi have dealings together," Bosco announced.

As soon as the words escaped his mouth, I shifted closer to the edge of my seat. If Bosco wasn't my brother, then he'd get a bullet through his head. Everyone knew I liked things to be investigated, with backgrounds triple checked.

"What are you saying?"

"Heath and Lucinda have a few dealings with the Russian mob. If we go in and make an effort to shut anything down, then it could hurt our business with Matevi." Bosco swept a hand around the room.

"Why am I just hearing of this news, Bosco?"

"I just got the news myself," Bosco replied.

"Too late to back out now," Armani informed us, standing and reaching for his gun.

Perhaps it's for the best. "So, he can't be touched."

"Not yet."

For a moment, I pondered whether I could avoid any blowback. "Get Penelope and if anyone hurts a hair on her head I will kill them."

I watched my brothers leave the room, then turned to stand and looked out at the afternoon skyline from the 30th floor. Business was smooth sailing for a while, only now things would get complicated—especially when Penelope became mine. My little dove has no idea what she does to me.

Nero had the role of keeping my mind on what was important and controlling my conscience whenever I tried to go rogue. "I never question your decisions," he said.

"Then don't start now."

"As your right-hand man and best friend, I would be a fool to not say that getting involved with her might bring on more drama." Nero rested a hand on the table.

"Since when do you hate drama? Nero, we've been running together since we were teenagers in Italy. Are you telling me you are scared now?"

"Never. Not a fool either."

I sighed, shoving my hands in my pockets. "I can't say I blame you."

"But you're still willing to kidnap her?"

"Yes."

"Then I'm by your side."

I stroked my chin. "If anyone becomes a problem..."

"Already know you want them to disappear." Nero trailed me to my office.

I bent down, shut off my computer, and picked up a few messages that were left by my assistant. I tossed my keys in my palm, leaving the office to head home and prepare for my new quest. Penelope staying at my main mansion in New Jersey would give us enough privacy and time to build on a lasting friendship.

Nero entered the limo on the right side. Banner started the ignition, waiting for me to duck in on the left. I called the landline to speak to my house manager.

"Mr. Calabresi," Maggie answered.

"Maggie, I'm coming in for the weekend and need to make sure everything is set for a guest."

"Is it the one you've explained would be a permanent guest?"

I gazed out of the window, then back to Nero on his phone. "Correct, you should have all of their favorite things from the list I sent you."

At first when I sprung the idea of Penelope moving into

my house, Maggie worried about our mafia life being too out in the open. We have guards around the clock, meetings where certain conversations could lead to death if repeated. If Penelope was able to get away and talked to the police, or spread our name in the wrong circles it could mean death. "Yes, the team got the list of items in the room and clothes."

"She might not be in the best of moods after the first few days, so be prepared."

"Understandable, Mr. Calabresi."

"Maggie, I shouldn't have to explain if anyone tries to interfere."

"No explanation is needed."

"Good. See you soon."

Maggie's been with me for the last five years handling all the home remodeling, decorating, and hiring staff. Everybody signed an NDA and backgrounds were checked before they were brought on as staff. I had my condo in the city and homes in Italy and Hawaii. For a few weeks, Penelope would hate being locked up, but it had to happen for her to get used to the life I have planned out.

* * *

"The moment she finds you, there's nothing you can do about your heart and head being constrained." Mother caressed my cheek.

I was staring into her eyes, lying my head in her lap at our home in Italy. At seventeen with a goal to follow in my father's footsteps, dating never worked. My parents argued constantly about me moving into that role, but ultimately, she wanted me to be happy, and even as a child, sitting in on meetings with my father and grandfather, I knew that family was the most important thing.

Giosuè

* * *

Memories of being in Italy were imprinted in my brain and gave me more energy to accomplish my next mission.

Chapter 4

Penelope

I snapped my fingers in the shower after a long night of dancing and drinking with my best friends. I was extremely glad I listened to Aspen and Lucy and went out to a party and let my hair down after a long week of school, dates, and dodging Lucinda's calls. Once I left the mansion, I made up my mind to finish school and move on from the escort life. I had enough saved up to get through the next few months of school, and hopefully an internship would lead to full-time work.

I finished scrubbing my skin, turned off the faucet, removed the towel from the back of the towel rack, and dried off. I tossed it in the hamper, still feeling a little tipsy from the drinks. I trekked to my adjoining bedroom, threw on a pair of bike shorts and a long t-shirt, and crawled into bed to relax and let the day ease from my mind.

* * *

"Shusshh."

Not even ten minutes into sleeping, and my eyes

popped open at the deep baritone voice. I screamed through the hand covering my mouth.

I reached up with a balled fist to punch him in the face, but he only tightened his grip and locked a hand around my wrists.

"I won't hurt you, but you are making it difficult with all of your thrashing."

"She's feisty."

My head whipped around at hearing another voice in the dark bedroom. I squirmed, trying to get away, and he scooped me off the bed. I kicked my legs. He put me in a bear hug and marched us out of the bedroom.

"He's going to owe us big time."

I perked up at his comment, while the two men in the front of my condo stared at my pictures.

How did they get in here? Where's security when you need them?

I paid too much money for a high-priced condo for security to not be on alert.

"Will you remain silent?" he asked me as tears pooled into my eyes.

"She can't run anywhere."

I looked over my shoulder at the man who was a few inches from me. Being placed on my feet, the taller guy released his hand from my mouth.

I stuttered, "I-I- won't say anything. Please, let me go."

"Sorry about this." I'd never met an apologetic kidnapper before.

Suddenly, I felt a pinch on my arm. Scared and panic, my eyes got low and darkness creeped in around me.

* * *

"He's going to be pissed."

"Who cares? At least we got her without a fight."

Slowly my eyes fluttered open. I felt heaviness like I'd taken a long nap. The only thing I remembered was going to sleep in my bed, and then someone was there.

"She's waking up."

A lump rose in my throat. I felt around the bed, my head snapping around at the voices. I blinked a few times, making out two men standing at the edge of a bed that was not mine.

I stared around the room, sat up on my knees, and covered up with the blanket. "I'm going to call the police."

Both men frowned at my statement. "Police?"

"I don't know how you got around the security in my building." My optimism was waning thin.

"Look around, Penelope. You're not home." The one with a sarcastic, raspy voice stood about six feet, with a beard, full lips and short black hair.

They looked familiar.

His friend, who stood a few inches taller, popped him on the shoulder. "Chill out, Armani."

The one called Armani grunted. "Why? She needs to know the truth."

Armani had a scrunched expression on his face.

I finally took in the dark curtains, large TV hanging on the wall, and framed artwork. My home would never amount to the expensive items in this bedroom. I gulped down the stress of trying to figure out how to get out of here. Maybe if I paid them off, they'd let me go without a problem. Moments like these I prayed my best friends would look into my disappearance if they didn't hear from me soon.

"I have money."

Both their heads angled to the right. "Do we look like we want your money?"

Suddenly, the door swung open to an older woman with gray hair in a tight bun holding a tray of food. I glared at her walking in like it was normal to kidnap someone.

"Armani, Bosco, give her some space."

"Maggie, she's talking about calling the police." The taller one stole a grape from the tray. Maggie reminded me of my grandmother. She placed it on the table in the corner, near the couch and next to the fireplace.

"She's scared, Bosco. You two need to get out." Maggie shooed them away, hands on her hips.

"Tell her the rules or he's going to be furious when I kill her," Armani announced. I stared at him knowing we would have a problem if I tried to escape.

Maggie shut the door behind them and slowly walked up the bed with a smile on her face. "I know you're scared, but I can promise he's not a bad person."

I ignored her statement, tossed the covers off my body, and stood, opening and closing drawers, searching for a phone. "I need a phone."

"Penelope, you are going to probably want to listen, so stay quiet before it becomes difficult."

"How do you people know my name?"

"My boss will explain it to you. Once you calm down, your stay here will be much easier."

"My stay?"

"My name is Maggie, I'm the house manager, boss—"

I ran to entrance of the bedroom and twisted the knob. It didn't open. I elevated my hand to bang on the door, and then on the wall, screaming for help. "I don't care."

A wedge of anger mixed with tears filled my throat.

"Help, I've been kidnapped."

Maggie held her hands in prayer form, begging, "Honey, please listen to me."

I hugged myself, wiped a hand down my face, and weighed my options of how to depart without getting killed. I felt like a caged animal locked away by strangers.

"Are you crazy? They kidnapped me! I want to go home."

She slowly walked up to me, and I stood with my hands up, warning her not to come closer.

"Penelope, I understand that your emotions are all over the place, but no one can help you."

I marched back over to the bed. "You are crazy."

Maggie gestured to the left corner. "I brought you breakfast and you have some clothes in the closet to change into."

"Can I please use the phone?" I felt my stomach sink.

"No, I can get you anything but that."

"Why are you doing this to me?"

She moved in a gentle, instinctive gesture of comfort. "He's a good person deep down."

"Who is he?!" I swallowed hard and squared my shoulders.

"Giosuè Calabresi—but if you attempt to contact the police or anyone outside his home, then I can't promise he will be so nice."

Maggie unlocked the door. It creaked open for her and she walked out. I jumped up and ran to try it again, but nothing happened. I pounded on the door over and over until tears ran down my cheeks. I tumbled to the floor, scared at what would happen to me.

"Giosuè Calabresi," I whispered my name to myself.

My stomach grumbled, but I refused to eat the food. I

slowly stood, walked to the window, and tried to pop open the lock.

I smacked my hand against the window, swiveled around, and pushed the tray of food off the table. My chest heaved up and down. "They kidnapped me." I ran to the bathroom and searched through the cabinets for anything I could use as a weapon. A few seconds went by, and a knock at the room door caused me to freeze. With each stride out of the bathroom, I kept my hands folded tight.

When I was younger, I'd been in a handful of fights; most girls thought that because I was quiet, they could try to bully me.

"Penelope, I—" Maggie stood in shock at the mess on the floor.

We made eye contact.

I slapped my hands together. "Tell this Giosuè person that he can go to hell. I know very important people, and if I'm not released right now, then he is going to regret that he ever met me."

A few staff members came in to clean up the food on the floor, not saying anything to me. I strolled over to the brass door and two tall burly men blocked me from leaving. Maggie talked with the two other housekeepers, and they picked up the last remaining plates and exited the space.

"I will send up some more food for you." Maggie gave me a warm smile and I snarled in return.

I wanted to scream, but it would get me nowhere.

* * *

For three days, the same routine happened, and my life felt like it was getting worse and worse. I refused to eat, and

Maggie would clean up whatever I shoved away. My anxiety was through the roof at being locked up 24/7, with no word of when I'd be let go. I glanced to the nightstand and picked off the note from the vase of flowers that were left.

In time, we will meet.

—Giosuè

It was the same flowers from my condo.

I crumbled up the note, ignoring the little contact he tried to make. Lucinda was probably going crazy wondering if I ran off on her.

Unless she's behind me getting kidnapped.

I usually spoke to Aspen and Lucy at least twice a day. It had to be Wednesday by now. I'd missed classes, and my professors would start reporting my absence.

There was a clicking sound. I glanced up from reading a book and the sexist man I'd ever seen walked into the room. He held no expression, but our eyes wouldn't leave each other.

"You've given my staff some problems." He wore a fitted charcoal-gray pinstriped suit, a watch on his left wrist, and gold cufflinks that accented his piercing green eyes.

My palms became sweaty; my breathing grew shallow, and my skin warmed at the intensity in his voice, which sent unease down my back. "Giosuè."

The huskiness lingered in his voice. "Are you hungry?"

"No, I want to go home."

"You are home."

I pointed at him. "It was you that had me brought here."

"Come downstairs, and we can talk." Giosuè whirled around and moved out of the bedroom.

I jumped out of bed, only wearing a pair of pajama pants and a thin spaghetti-strap tank top. I trudged out of the room and paused at the long, wide hallway decorated in maroon, black, and silver. The place was massive. I looked down the staircase and saw a few people carrying flowers in and out of the house. The jiggle of keys announced that someone was entering, and I could have tried to run out, but I might have gotten killed in the process—however, at the moment, I'd rather be dead than locked in an unfamiliar place, waiting to be killed or assaulted.

"You can try to escape, but you won't get far." I spun around to the left to Armani petting the side of his waist, which probably held a gun. I rolled my eyes and headed downstairs, brushing a hand up and down my arms. Giosuè's home wasn't just a mansion; it was like a castle, with wide doors and windows draped in dark colors, large chandeliers hanging from the ceiling, high-priced art on the walls, and a simple railing with a wraparound veranda. As I went down the hallway, I bypassed at least ten doors, and men stood at each corner with no expression. I knew that no friendliness or help would come from them.

"He's waiting for you." Maggie popped out and motioned to the open room floor. The entrance steps led down into a cream decorated dining room.

The sight of enough food to feed an army caught my attention as I stepped downstairs.

"I hope you're hungry. The chef wanted to make all

your favorite foods." Giosuè picked up his napkin, sitting at the head of the table.

How did he know baked potatoes, pasta, and crab boils were my favorite?

I assumed that the place setting next to him was my seat, but I defied him and sat at the opposite end of the table.

He chuckled, showing a bright smile that made me tingle in a way I should not. *Get it together, the man had you kidnapped.*

"I want to go home."

"Come here, Penelope."

"No."

His soothing voice probed further. "Has my hospitality not been up to your standards?"

My eyes narrowed at his remark. Did he think I wanted to be here?

"Kidnapping women is a crime."

Giosuè sipped his drink. "A crime?"

"Yes, you have no idea the people I know that will have you arrested." My time in law school had prepared me for life-or-death situations.

Speaking viciously, he asked, "Who? Lucinda or Heath?"

My eyes rose wide in shock. "Lucinda is behind you taking me?" I leaned my hands flat on the table.

Between the lack of sleep, and the people running in and out of the room, trying to make me comfortable, I had to know if she really was a cold-hearted bitch who was only after money.

Giosuè stabbed his fork into his food. "Eat your food."

"I'm not hungry. You've kept me locked up for days, and my family is probably searching for me."

"Eat, Penelope." He ignored my comment.

"No!" I jumped up and slammed my hand on the table.

"Penelope Hutton, twenty-five years old, law-school student at Columbia University. Your grandmother passed away when you were sixteen and your parents abandoned you when you were a baby. You're currently making money as one of Lucinda's high-profile escorts."

My mouth dropped open in awe.

How is it possible? Who is this man?

"Eat and we can talk."

It was impossible to steady my erratic pulse. "It was you following me."

He paused and smirked. "Little Dove, I am a man that usually keeps things buttoned up, but you caught my attention."

"I'd rather you ignored me."

He laughed. Giosuè's broad shoulders hunched under his laughter. "My brothers are right, you're feisty."

"How long will you continue to keep me here?"

"Eat, Penelope. I know you've skipped a few meals. Maggie keeps me updated."

"Are you expecting sex? I mean, you're feeding and clothing me. What are you expecting, Mr. Calabresi? As a client of Lucinda's, you only get dinner and a few hugs for a specific price."

His classically handsome features seared into me. "Little Dove, I have very little patience."

"That makes two of us. And why are you calling me Little Dove?" I spat.

"Sit down and eat or go back to your room."

A loud rumble could be heard coming from my stomach at that moment. He was right about one thing: I hadn't really eaten since being here. Not knowing their true intentions, I had been worried that they would try to poison me.

"How do I know you're not trying to kill me?"

"I brought you here. If I wanted you dead, then I could have saved my time and money and left you for dead at your home."

The words scraped my throat. "Tell me why I'm here."

"I have some information that Lucinda was going to snatch you up."

"Lucinda's not stupid. I make her a lot of money and the clients would never let her hurt me."

"Lucinda's business and mine have crossed paths a few times, and I came across you, along with one of her clients who is in my way."

"Who?"

"Heath Laurier."

"Heath? And how am I in the way?" I dropped down in the chair, confused.

"I don't share."

I snatched up the glass of water and tossed it across the room. "I don't belong to you or anyone else!"

Giosuè had an air of authority and the appearance of someone who demanded instant obedience. "Do you intend to eat?"

I jumped up balled my fists. "Fuck your food, Giosuè!"

My blood boiled with him giving me these half-assed answers. I'd appreciate a straight answer so I could get the hell out of here. Him bringing up Heath and Lucinda made it even more suspicious; it seemed like all three of them were into some weird shit.

"Lucinda has her hands in human trafficking."

I knew she was dangerous, but not into selling women.

"Only way you know is because you've bought women from her."

"I have some businesses that have crossed those lines, but we've worked hard on getting out of that line of funds."

I stood motionless in the middle of the room. "Can you tell me how long you plan on locking me up?"

"You're free to move around, but only with people I trust."

"Those two guys that took me."

"My brothers."

I sauntered two chairs down and grabbed a plate, adding some fruit, toast, and eggs to it, and took a seat.

"Armani and Bosco." With a full plate I settled into the deep red cushions.

Giosuè nodded in answer. "Did they hurt you?"

"I mean, if you think kidnapping is a normal thing, then I guess not. What was in the needle?"

His mouth thinned in displeasure. "Needle?"

"Yeah, one of them stabbed me with something, but when I woke up, I couldn't remember whether I was dreaming or not."

"I apologize about that. I told them to take care of you."

"Can I call my friends?" I managed to ask through stiff lips.

We made eye contact for a few seconds and then he shook his head left to right. "Not yet."

"I promise to not escape. If you know my life, then you know that school is important to me, Giosuè."

"We have your books and I spoke with your professors."

My face went grim. "How?" For him to get in touch with my professors, let alone Lucinda, showed he was someone with a lot of money to get what he wants.

"I have connections at Columbia. You won't fail."

If there was ever a time to hold back my true thoughts, it would be now, but I never went with my first thoughts. "Are you crazy?"

"Yes."

"Wow. At least you are honest."

After wiping his mouth with the napkin in his hand, Giosuè smiled, rose from the table, and came around to stand next to me with his hand out for me to take.

Something about the look in his eyes made me want to lower my coldness.

One corner of his mouth shifted upward. "I promise to let you talk to your friends if you come with me."

"Where are we going?"

"I would like for you to put on some clothes. The men working around my estate should never be able to see your body."

I jerked my neck back in anger. "These are clothes." There's nothing worse than someone who felt they could control what you wore. He reminded me of all the men I had met in my life who put their opinions on my decisions.

"Lil' Dove, that mouth of yours will have you in trouble."

I pulled away from his grip on my chin. A man like him probably hated to be challenged.

"I want to show you something." His hand fell on my lower back, leading me out of the dining area and across the hall to an office. Giosuè opened the door, and I froze, seeing Armani and Bosco sitting at his desk with another man.

"How many times do I have to tell you to get your feet off my desk, Armani?" Giosuè smacked his feet down and took a seat at his desk.

I stood toward the back of the room.

Giosuè gestured to his family. "Penelope, you met my

brothers, Bosco and Armani. The quiet one that's smiling is my best friend, Nero."

The one he called Nero chucked his chin up at me.

"She seems nicer today," Armani commented, and I wanted to strike him in the face.

"Armani." Giosuè's expression was a mask of stone.

I preferred to be anywhere but here, but I could already tell he had a lot of security. "You seem crazier today."

Bosco, Nero, and Giosuè all chuckled at my reply.

"Nice to see you again, Penelope. I am sorry for snatching you up," Bosco said. Nero raised his hand and smacked him on the back of the head.

Giosuè logged into his computer, then waved me over to his desk. I hesitated, fidgeted on one foot, and glanced over my shoulder.

Make a run for it, Penelope.

"I promise you won't get far." Armani ground the words out between his teeth.

I pressed my lips shut, resisting with every means in my body to ignore him.

Armani had better keep his gun away from my reach because the moment I had a chance to use it, he'd be the first person on my list.

Chapter 5

Giosuè

Penelope was still unsure about me, and I had no right to ask for her trust. But she needed the information, so she would know that Lucinda was not someone she should rely on. Even though I took her from her home, I would never hurt her. I only wanted to protect what's mine. She and Armani had some type of hate for each other that needed to be resolved because she wasn't going anywhere. I knew my little brother hated anyone being this close to us, but she was more than a woman I spotted out and would take back to a hotel. Penelope had a hold on me from the first time I saw her sitting with a man at the bar laughing and talking. Those oval shaped eyes and bright smile, and wild fiery red hair forced me to rethink everything I thought when it came to relationships. I clicked on the computer for the volume, motioning for Penelope to come closer. Nero closed us in. Bosco sat up and clenched his fist at the sounds of rustling that emerged from the recording he got from his people.

"I want her picked up. I am losing too much money."

"She's not going to be easy, Lucinda."

"*I know, but Heath is planning to pay me half of the money that I could make if she went to Dubai.*"

"*What if he finds out?*"

"*I have other girls that can replace her.*"

"*And Giosuè?*"

"*He thinks I will let him swoop in to buy my business and thinks he can't be touched.*"

"*Are we going to war with him?*"

"*Giosuè will lose interest fast. The twenty million I get from the Russian buyer, plus telling Heath that Giosuè is the reason for Penelope going missing will kill two birds with one stone.*"

Penelope covered her mouth in a loud gasp. I paused the recording and let those words pass through the room so she would understand I wasn't the bad guy. A feeling of having to hold her close and not let go filled my head.

"I can't believe she would do something so vile."

A gust of her scent lingered and quickly distracted me from the current task.

"She's pissed about you quitting. I won't say I was happy to know that wealthy men paid to go out with you, but from the research I have done, you never slept around."

Armani scoffed and I glared at him.

Penelope placed her palm on her stomach and mouth. "I think I'm going to be sick."

I rushed to open the bathroom door in the corner and pulled out the extra toothbrush and left on the counter. I gave her some privacy and stepped out of the way with her bent over the toilet, puking up the little food she'd eaten at breakfast.

"I have to meet with Matevi," Bosco reminded me, standing up.

We all had a room in each other's home. They had properties a mile away, also behind gated walls.

The faucet turned on a few seconds later. When Penelope returned, she appeared a little flushed.

"I need to speak with my friends."

A decent man would allow her to leave to figure things with the police, but I'm not decent. "Give me a minute to sort out the details with my brother."

"Does Lucinda know you took me?"

"She probably will by now. We went to the mansion first and she said you'd left before we'd arrived."

"Heath... Is he still alive?" There appeared to be care in her tone.

"He's of no concern, Penelope."

She drew a deep breath. "Why do you—"

I thrusted my hand to halt the question. I understood having doubts, but her protection was what I would never lack on. "Bosco, take Nero with you."

"Since when does Bosco go out in the field without me?" Armani pinched his nose in aggravation.

"I need you to get surveillance on Lucinda and who she's trying to sell Penelope to."

Armani glowered at me for a brief moment, then stuck his hand out for me to take, and that was our way of coming to terms with each other without getting into an argument. At the end of the day, I was the boss, and he was the enforcer; questioning me would not be tolerated—brother or not.

All three of them left, and Penelope stood at the window, staring out sadly.

"Being here is new."

"Am I supposed to be grateful to be kidnapped before I

was sold off to some foreign country?" she spat, her nostrils flaring.

"Grateful? No, I imagine you're pissed all around, but my home is comfortable and spacious."

She swung around, not waiting for an answer. "You've been stalking me. The flowers at my condo. The car at my school."

"Yes, it's true."

"Why? I mean, how old are you?"

"Thirty-seven. I never planned on making contact this early."

She pressed her back against the wall. "What do you want?"

Surrounded by her delicate yet provocative sensuousness and disarming personality gave me strength and weakness combined. "At the moment, your time."

"Pretty sure you can find a woman to spend time with, so why me?"

"Lil' Dove you're special."

Her steps shifted, and her middle finger stabbed the desk. "Stop calling me Dove."

"You are special, sweet, delicate like a dove."

"A man like you is angry, arrogant, and an asshole that feels like they can do anything they want and not answer to police."

I laughed at her correct assumption. "Call your friends. I'm not worried about you trying to call the police." I stuck my hand in my pants pocket to remove my phone, then held it up at her.

"Why is that?"

"Calabresi owns the police."

Penelope's hand grazed against mine and a spark

punched me in the gut. I let it go and veered away to give her some privacy.

"You really going to leave me in here alone?"

"The situation is what you make it, Penelope."

"Giosuè. I can't imagine any woman in your life okay with you taking me from my home."

I paused at the entryway with my hand on the wall. "My sister would disagree."

"If I get out of here, I will kill you."

I nodded. Not looking back at her, my footsteps thundered down the hall and into the kitchen. I yanked the fridge wide open, pulled out a bottled water, and gulped it down. Maggie gave directions to the cooking staff, then turned to me with a frown.

"I recall that exact grimace when I bought this house."

"Well, I told you it was too much house for just you." Maggie gazed around the kitchen, waving her hand in the air.

I leaned against the island. "Tell me your thoughts."

Maggie crossed her arms. "She's young."

"Penelope's different." Me being a violent man, one would think Maggie was crazy for sticking with me for so many years, but she often said her vested interest in making me good would pay off one day.

Maggie's left brow lifted up. "And Tinsley?"

"Tinsley means nothing to me."

Maggie picked up the towel on the island, wiping it down. "Hopefully she knows that because I like Penelope for you." Maggie poured soap on the sponge to clean the stove. Most of the staff lived on site like the butler, maid, and Maggie.

"Armani hates I brought her here."

Maggie rinsed the sponge under the water, then cleaned

her hands. "Armani needs to find love. His cold heart keeps everybody at a distance."

I chuckled. "Except you."

Maggie became the somewhat surrogate mother in our lives. The person to give us advice. "All three of you mean a lot to me. Dinner tonight will be your favorite."

I pushed off the island. "Actually, I plan on taking Penelope out."

"A date? You never go on dates." Maggie held tight glee in her eyes.

I started toward my entryway. "I've held her inside long enough. Lucinda won't make a move now."

Maggie slowed her steps. "Be careful with her. From what you told me, she's been through a lot."

"Thanks, Maggie." I left the kitchen and shuffled up my office, pressing my ear to the door to listen.

"I don't have time, Aspen. Listen to me," Penelope barked harshly.

"Some guys kidnapped me—hello, Aspen, can you hear me?"

The phone call was being recorded, and when certain words were used, I had set it to hang up. Penelope thought she could sneak around and give away details of what had happened, but I had it all arranged. I pushed forward to step inside and she froze, hanging up the phone, and glared at me.

"I hope your call went well."

Her mind and body were in a standoff. She moved her hand to her hip. "Did you do something to my friends?"

"Why do you ask?"

"The call dropped and I know Aspen is worried about me."

"You can see your friends soon, Penelope."

"Is this all a business transaction or some stupid game? Why not let me go with Lucinda? I can get the police to support me."

"Because I have plans for you." I deliberately didn't answer her comment about the police. With my connections, Lucinda would easily be locked up, but it might cause more questions about my business, and we needed the ports clear and new logistics for the garage pickup. She threw her hands skyward and marched past me. I reached out to grip her elbow. "We have dinner reservations."

A look of defiance alerted me to let her go.

"And if I want to skip your plans?"

"Not possible."

Penelope slammed the phone down. "So, you're forcing yourself on me."

"Get dressed. We'll leave in an hour." I let the frustration and anger she was taking out on my office roll off my back.

"Let me go."

"Penelope."

"Anything else, Mr. Calabresi?"

"No, Penelope Hutton."

* * *

I rented out Le Cruz's restaurant, Opulent Designs, an elite French refined seafood place, near W. 51st in proximity to Radio Center Music Hall and the art museum. Penelope was quiet on the way and kept close to the window, avoiding my stare. As soon as we sat down the waitress brought us a white chardonnay.

Her uniqueness was alluring, her slender but voluptuous body natural in the silky gown.

"How are your studies going?"

Penelope drank her glass of wine. "I wouldn't know since I've missed my tests."

"I spoke with your professors, and you can make up the tests."

"On campus?"

"No."

Penelope forcefully banged her wine glass on the tabletop and sent a few drops spilling onto her hand. "What are you looking to get from me?"

I extended my napkin to assist her in cleaning off her hand. "What specifically are you intending to pursue a career as a lawyer for?" Although the roaring guests covered our conversation, I still heard some of her voice.

"Something tells me you already know."

I curved my lip upwards. "Humor me."

"Family Law."

"That's commendable."

"Well, after being abandoned and then losing my grandmother at sixteen, I was bounced around in foster care until I was eighteen."

"Do you know what happened to your parents or if they're alive still?"

"No, my grandmother avoided any conversation about my parents."

"Understandable. She wanted to keep your innocence."

She scoffed. The waitress arrived with our meals and placed them on the table. "Tell me the truth, are you dating someone?" The question seemed to intrigue her.

"No."

"So, no girlfriend, wife, or sneaky link?"

"Sneaky link?" My mind drifted to Tinsley.

Penelope savored the food in her mouth. "A man like

you has plenty of women falling at your feet to be with you."

I recognized a need to keep her talking. "Work is my sneaky link." The harder she tried to ignore looking at me, the easier it became to plan my steps with Lucinda, then Heath.

"Liar."

"I wanted to avoid you at first, so I kept my distance."

"That's why men have followed me around and left flowers at the hotel."

"For your protection."

Penelope leaned forward, arms on the table. "Protection? My life was fine before you interrupted it." Penelope took her fork and knife and cut into her beef bourguignon.

"Finish eating."

"I'd rather go home." A heaviness centered on her face.

I watched her finish her meal then waved for the waitress to bring to-go boxes. After paying, I stood and drifted to her, pulled out her chair to help her stand, and gripped her by the palm. We strolled out of the restaurant, and she snatched herself away from my grip, searching up and down the street.

"There's nowhere to run. I have people at every corner, Penelope."

"Where are you taking me?"

I guided her back to the car. "You will see."

Macsen stopped in front of us, and I helped her inside and closed the door behind us, motioning for him to drive to the next destination. It was a smooth ride. As we coasted in and out of traffic, bright lights beamed across buildings, right up to the gallery. Part of my investments were in art—not only to make money but because of a passion that my mother had put into my life.

I shut the fridge and trekked out to the hall to see a light on in the den. "Mom, what are you doing up so late?" I asked, peering at her sitting down with large art books on the table.

"Come sit down, Giosuè."

I yawned and plopped down next to her on the couch. "What are you doing?"

"I am thinking of some new pieces for the house."

"Pieces of junk." I chuckled and she pinched me on the arm.

She pointed at pictures of men and women dressed in gowns. "No, my darling. Art. Something you think is junk could be the most expensive item to a country." She grinned.

The staff stood outside to escort us in for a private showing of the latest items that had recently shipped in from Italy and London.

When she reached the entrance, Penelope did a quick scan around the front. "What are we doing here?"

"I'd like to tell you a little bit about myself."

Penelope took a step towards the wall of paintings encased near the door.

"You collect art?"

"I do. This is one aspect of my business."

"I'm surprised you know something about art."

"What? I don't look like the type to appreciate pieces of art?"

Penelope edged closer to the Picasso in the distant corner. "You don't."

"Mr. Calabresi. Can we speak in the back, please?" Ruiz, the manager of the gallery, approached me. I looked over at Penelope engulfed in the painting of a naked woman lying on a bed.

Ruiz stepped around to his desk, pulled up the reports on his laptop, and I glanced at the documents.

"Has Bosco seen the numbers?"

Ruiz hit the print key. "Not yet. I went through it twice."

"For the first shipment, we had no problems."

Ruiz piled the papers together. "I understand. Armani watched the load come in and leave, so we should see a consistent amount."

"The new routes are coming in soon and we can add to these numbers."

Ruiz typed on the keyboard and logged out. "Great. I will keep you updated."

"Let me get back out here."

"Is she the one?" Ruiz had worked for me a few years, but he'd never seen me bring anyone to my family's business before.

"You never know."

Ruiz had worked for us in Italy before I brought him to the States to help run our local businesses as the accountant. There were very few people whom I trusted and I'd had him come out of retirement to work for me.

Penelope laughed among the other staff. When I came up beside her she acted like I was the devil and closed her mouth, shifting back to her conversation with my team. Even though she held contempt for the way I brought her in my life, I appreciated the way she forced herself to have a nice evening. I promised I wouldn't make a bold move unless she opened up to me more. Even with her talking to her friend, Aspen, I still had her on a tightrope with not leaving my side. I knew she'd had a few internship interviews that she was waiting to hear back from, and I had a family member who was a lawyer with one of their firms in New York. I made it my mission to get her in to work with the best. Elio would be flying in soon for a quick business trip and I planned for them to talk. I eased my hand to her lower back, still amazed at the soft curves in the ivory dress that wrapped around her waist with a cutout in the center showing her full breasts, luring me to lick and suck them into my mouth.

"Are you ready to go?"

Pop! Pop!

Loud gunshots echoed around us. Penelope screamed and squatted down holding her ears. I pulled her behind me near the wall a few feet from the door. Macsen was parked out front. I pulled out my gun and directed my bodyguards to split up. Penelope clenched her hands on my jacket tightly.

Pop! Pop!

"Arghhhh!" Penelope screamed, trying to run out the back toward the exit for employees, but I clasped a hand around her waist.

Pop! Pop!

I raised her chin and forced her to look at me. "Shusshhh... Penelope, listen to me."

"I want to go home," she begged, shivering against my chest.

"Trust me. When I count to three, we're going to head out to the limo."

Penelope's eyes widened in fear. "I can't."

I glanced to the left and saw Macsen waving for us to come out. "You can and will. Follow my lead."

Penelope shook her head again, struggling to move.

"One. Two. Three." I jumped up and ran outside with my gun pointed high—ready to kill anyone I didn't know.

Penelope sprinted to the car, climbed in, and shut the door. After I made sure she was secure and scanned the scene, I sprinted to the passenger side and noticed a body positioned dead center of the street.

"Who do you think he's working for?" Macsen asked.

"No clue, either Lucinda or the Russians."

Macsen held up his phone to show me a text message. "Armani said he can meet you at the house."

"Not tonight. Penelope's distraught. In the morning we'll talk. Inform Bosco that we will cut the ports if Matevi has any connection with tonight," I announced. Macsen brought the phone to his ear, made a call, and got in the car taking us back to the mansion.

Slowly, I helped Penelope sit up. Once we cleared the streets, we heard police sirens floating by us, and I reached into my coat sleeve to dial my contact.

"I heard."

"Foster, make sure that it doesn't get traced back to me."

"The gallery was closed, correct?" Foster probed.

Exhaustion seemed to seep across Penelope's face as she wiped it clear of the tears that wouldn't stop falling down her cheeks.

"Someone must have been following me. I will handle any footage, just keep it quiet coming from any police wires."

He grumbled. "Only have the ability to do so much from my position."

"You know me, Foster. Being in the DEA is only helpful to a point," I snapped.

"I know and I need to avoid having you as much as I can from being on DEA inquiries on your business."

"Like it never happened, Foster."

Penelope's head swiveled when I made my comment.

Foster Raynor came to one of our clubs a few years back with information about my name coming up from a snitch about to spill on where we keep our product, our locations, and the times we did pickups. Initially, I didn't believe him because it seemed out of the blue for an agent to warn us. We checked him for a wire and ran a background check before having a real meeting with my brothers and Nero. Once he brought more tips on police or any other agency trying to come down on us, I paid him a healthy fee.

"The ports will have extra security over the next few days, so keep your people away."

Before he could reply, I clicked to disconnect and dropped my phone in my pocket, gazing back at Penelope.

"Sorry about tonight."

She didn't reply, only turned away from me to the window while the vehicle moved through the gates of my home.

The thick tension in the car left me worried. Would this keep her closed off before we really got started? I rubbed a hand down my face and unbuttoned my coat when we made it back home. Silence lengthened between us. Macsen helped Penelope get in the house and I stayed back, staring at the home I built.

I slipped off my trench coat and suit jacket. Maggie trekked down the hall from the kitchen and met me at the edge of the staircase.

"How was your date?"

Penelope stayed quiet; her face flushed.

"There was a shooting."

"Are you hurt? Do you think it's a good idea to continue?"

I pressed a kiss on her cheek and headed upstairs to my bedroom. "I have no choice."

Chapter 6

Penelope

I could have been killed. It had been running over and over in my brain since the night of the shooting. I sat in the chair of my professor's office waiting for them to arrive. Macsen had been right by my side; the only way I could get a fraction of my previous life back was to agree to a one-on-one teaching method. Giosuè must have threatened the professor's life in some capacity; the only way to get word to Aspen was to try to talk with the professor alone. Macsen stood beside the door, and I smiled and waited, a nervousness bursting inside me as I formulated my escape plan.

Those gunshots only made it clear that being anywhere near Giosuè Calabresi would end up with me dead or in the hospital. Honestly, it was no better than being with Lucinda or Heath.

Taking a step in his office, Professor Williams leaned forward and pushed his glasses up on his nose, then plopped down in his chair. "Miss Hutton, thank you for waiting."

"Professor Williams, thank you for meeting with me

about my grades." I was too close to being finished to have anything interrupt it.

"My normal teaching method will be condensed for time. I have compiled a listing of books you can check for studying form the library."

I dipped my hand in my purse to retrieve my pen for notes. "I apologize again for what has happened."

"No need. You only missed one test, so for now we can get you caught up. I have a packet for you for the rest of the semester."

"But—"

Professor Williams shot a glance at Macsen, inclined his head sideways, removed his glasses, and exhaled a long breath. "Miss Hutton, we only have an hour before my next class."

I flexed my hands on my thighs and cocked my head from left to right. "Macsen, do you mind giving us privacy?"

Macsen answered, "Mr. Calabresi stated to not leave you alone."

I bit my bottom lip, flipped over my notebook, and took the test from Professor Williams' hand. Below my book, I pulled out a note that I hoped the professor would keep private.

"You have thirty minutes to read the information. We'll go over the packet."

"Okay."

Taking my time with each question, I carefully read it. Some of the questions weren't too difficult seeing as I'd already read up on each section before I was taken. Professor Williams sat reading a book. I laid the pen down on the desk.

"Are you finished with the exam?" he asked.

I handed in my test.

Usually, the hallway filled up around this time, and I needed it to be clear if I wanted to make an escape.

I held a hand up to my mouth to cough. "Professor, do you mind if I run to the restroom?"

"Mr. Calabresi stated you should not leave the room." Macsen moved in closer, and I released a breath, making eye contact with Professor Williams.

"Um, the bathroom is two doors down. It's probably safe right now since it's empty."

The professor caught on to my suggestion, and I mouthed thank you.

"Hurry right back. I'm watching," Macsen explained, and I turned to walk out of the room. Macsen stood watching me from the hallway. In an effort to prove I wasn't lying, I looked behind me, smiled, and pointed to the bathroom door.

As I started to pull it open, someone came out and stepped to the side, giving me space. Hurriedly, I locked it behind me and paced back and forth thinking.

"The window."

Thankfully, the professor's office was on the main floor, and the window wasn't locked. I pulled the trashcan over, hopped on top, and pushed it open. I stared out of the window, not seeing any more guards.

"You can do it, Penelope," I muttered to myself.

As soon as I crawled through, I heard a knock. "Shit." I fell on the ground, jumped up, wiping the dirt from my pants, and latched the window back. I sprinted to the side of the building, hoping that Macsen hadn't come in to notice that I was gone.

I raked a hand across my forehead. "Think, Penelope."

Normally, around eleven, Aspen was in class, and going back to my condo wouldn't work. I took off my coat, let my hair down from my ponytail, and jogged through the grass. I scanned the parking lot and saw Alden arriving for class with a few friends. He smiled when he noticed me. Ordinarily, I would have turned him away, but right now, he was the only person who could help.

My heart thrummed in my chest. "Alden, you have to help me."

"Penelope, I thought you were avoiding me." Alden tangled his thumb around a lock of my hair.

I raised my hand to knock it down. "Look, we don't have much time. Can we go somewhere and talk?"

"Penelope!" Macsen's voice echoed loudly.

It felt like my stomach was hollowing out at the loud roar of my name. I spun around. "Shit. Please let's go."

Alden started to move around to confront Macsen. "Who is that?"

Macsen held up his phone, then sprinted toward the parking lot. I snatched the keys from Alden's hand and ran to his car as he trailed beside me.

"Hey! My car!" He opened the door and climbed in. I haphazardly reversed from the spot, not letting him close the door.

Macsen removed his gun. "Penelope!"

"He has a gun!" Alden screamed.

I stepped on the gas, not looking back, trying to think of a way to get out of the city. I blew through a stop sign. "Let me see your phone."

A car horn went off beside us.

"Penelope, pull over." Alden finally had his seatbelt locked.

I held my hand to his face. "Alden, you have to listen to me."

"You're acting crazy."

I slammed my hand on the wheel. "I was kidnapped!" Throughout our whole relationship, Alden had never really made me feel protected as his woman. He lacked in all areas, and me being young and stupid, I let it go on for too long. Sometimes, it had become like high school, with women making statements on how we weren't a real couple, and there were pictures of him with other girls. Now here I was in a car chase and he's the one I had to ask for help.

Alden's brows bunched together. "What?"

"The man back there works for a guy named Giosuè Calabresi."

"Calabresi? That name seems familiar." Alden twisted in his seat to face me.

"Because he's a mafia boss."

Alden's eyes rose in surprise. "Mafia!"

"I know but listen—we have to get out of the city."

Alden stretched his hand out to grip the steering wheel, and I pushed his shoulder for him to move back. "Are you crazy? Take me home."

Finally, we got on the main street, and I arrived at a red light. "Not that simple. If they know where I live, they more than likely have your address."

Alden's jaw set hard, and he glowered at me. "No. We need to go to the police."

"The police." The light changed to green and I moved with row of cars ahead, thinking of his comment.

"My uncle can probably help. He's retired but knows a few people."

"I don't know." I swerved in and out of traffic, making it close to Pershing Square. Stopping at Fifth Avenue, rain started to pour down. The light turned green, and I eased my speed to turn down 40th Street when a car pulled in front and blocked me.

In a bid to catch his attention, I slumped in the chair, chin tucked low in the seat. "Alden."

"Penelope, who the fuck is this guy?" Alden dug his teeth into his lip.

"Run," I muttered, reached down, and unlocked the door.

Alden yelled my name, his chest heaving up and down. I saw Macsen yank Alden out of the car, holding a gun to his head.

I stopped running. "No!" I shouted, shoving two men away from me, but they held me up.

"Mr. Calabresi wants you to come quietly and he won't hurt your friend."

I snatched myself out of the guard's tight hold. "Why are you doing this to me?"

"He's in the car waiting on you to make a decision."

"I-I-" I stammered, taking in the scene I made.

Pop

"Penelope!" Alden's body jerked back, and my eyes rose in shock. I bit down on one of the guards' arms and ran over to Alden. I ran to help him, to see him shot in front of me was heartbreaking.

"What the fuck!" he screamed and shoved me away.

The two of us weren't together anymore, but he didn't deserve to die. I cupped his head, holding my left hand on his chest.

I begged, mouth in a straight line. "Alden, hold on." Blood continued to spread. My throat became achingly thick. Everyone around me just stood there.

Macsen squatted to his knees. "Penelope, we need to go."

I ignored him. "Alden, keep breathing. The ambulance is coming."

Out the side of my eye I saw Macsen motion to another guard to come closer.

A pair of strong hands wrapped around my waist and tugged me off Alden, kicking and screaming.

Giosuè bellowed, "Let her go!"

He stopped and dropped me on the ground, and I curled up in a ball.

"He's going to be all right. I have to get you to safety," Giosuè commanded.

I balled up my fist to hit him, and he held both arms down by my sides. "Help! Call the police!" Tears flowed down my cheeks as I shouted.

Giosuè marched to his car and placed my back against the door, forcing us to face each other.

"No! Let me go."

Pressing his forehead to mine, Giosuè commanded, "Penelope, listen to me."

"Boss."

I choked back a cry, frightened at what I'd done. "He's going to kill me!"

Giosuè finally dragged me into the backseat. I slammed my hand on the window and screamed at the top of my lungs. Macsen and a few other men helped Alden to another truck farther away. I pounded on the window and door to be released, but the child lock was on.

"Bosco, track down who took that shot," Giosuè demanded.

Giosuè reached down to touch my leg, and I crawled away from him. "No, stay away from me."

"Penelope, you have to calm down."

The limo backed up and pulled off.

"You killed him," I whispered, feeling lightheaded. My eyes fluttered rapidly until darkness enveloped me.

* * *

When I suddenly jumped up, I awoke with a horrible nightmare of Alden being killed right before my eyes. I flicked on the light on my nightstand and was surprised to see Giosuè sitting in the chair and staring back at me.

I dragged the comforter up my chest. "How did I get here?"

"How are you feeling?" Giosuè watched me with an acute, hard stare.

"I had a nightmare. What am I doing in bed?"

"Are you hungry?"

I shoved the cover back, started to get out of bed, and my stomach grumbled. "I am—but wait. My nightmare felt real."

Giosuè stood and strode to leave. "Maggie cooked dinner. I have to go out."

I staggered to stand up straight, but I felt dizzy. I sat back on the bed. "Hold up, Professor Williams, I took a test and then... Alden."

"He's not dead." There was a cold edge to his voice, like it would have been better if they did kill him.

"So, it's true." Numbness consumed me. Alden was shot for real.

Giosuè swiftly moved to tower over me. "You tried to escape and someone tried to kill you and they shot Alden instead."

I hugged myself. "Tried to kill me? No, they were aiming for him." I pushed back the hair that had fallen in my face. "Mr. Calabresi."

"Giosuè," he corrected me.

I held up my palms. "Giosuè, I apologize for trying to leave, but Alden is innocent."

"He's your boyfriend."

"Ex-boyfriend." I crawled and rose out of bed. I caught Giosuè by the right hand to stop him from leaving the room. "Okay, do you want to sleep with me? Is that what all this is about?"

Giosuè jerked his hand away. He slammed the door shut, pushed me back against the wall, and extended his hand to grip my chin. "One thing you will do is show me respect."

"You kidnapped me!"

He pressed his leg in between mine, lips an inch from my mouth. "I saved your life." He wore a stern expression.

"For your own selfish reasons."

The devilish gleam in his eyes held more than desire and lust. It was like he was seeing me for the first time ever. Giosuè was a beautiful older man, but the way he put demands on my life would never work for me.

"Selfish reasons?"

"You stalked me for months, and you think I will just be grateful?" I scoffed.

Slowly he caressed my cheek with the back of his hand. "Relationships aren't my thing, but you intrigue me, Penelope."

"Find someone else to intrigue you. You hurt someone."

He grinned. "Eat. I have some business to handle."

"No, I am not eating until you bring my friends and Alden."

Giosuè released me, taking a step back. "Demanding won't work with me, Little Dove."

"Stop calling me that!" I planted my hands on his chest, shoving him backwards.

Giosuè put his hands up in surrender and nodded. "I

have watched you to keep you safe, and I won't apologize anymore. You should thank me for not killing your ex."

I yelled to his back, "You're disgusting!"

He slammed the door and I stomped to the nightstand, gripped the lamp, and tossed it to the wall in anger. Aspen and Lucy had no idea what I'd been through and I was praying Alden could call the police to get me out of here. I strode to the bathroom, turned on the shower, and pinned my hair in a bun. I would have a hard time convincing Giosuè to let me leave again after this morning—and sneaking in a call would be worse.

At this point, if he killed me, I would welcome the freedom of being out of his life.

Finally, I went downstairs after showering and walked into the kitchen to find Maggie talking with Giosuè's brother.

"Well, hello. How are you feeling, Penelope?" Maggie asked.

I fumbled with my hands. "Fine. Giosuè said lunch was ready."

"Yes, I had them make some soup," Maggie commented, gesturing to the pot on the stove.

"Thanks."

"Giosuè usually dislikes when someone disobeys him. You made an impression on him."

"He's an asshole."

Bosco bent over in laughter. "I like you."

I sat at the island, scooped some of the soup on a spoon, and blew out a breath to cool it down. "Can't say the same."

"Normally we sit in the dining room," Maggie informed me, cutting up pieces of bread and piling them on a plate.

"The table's too big to sit at it alone. Where's Giosuè?"

"Look at you, asking about your man." Bosco stood,

carried his bowl to the sink, turned on the faucet, rinsed it off, and leaned with his back on the countertop.

"What's your name again?" I ate more of the tomato soup and picked up the bread to dunk in it.

He answered, "Bosco."

"Bosco, how is Alden doing?"

Maggie and Bosco made eye contact. "Penelope, do you want water with your soup or tea?" Maggie tried to change the subject.

"Water, please."

Maggie poured water from the jug into a glass. "I heard you're going to be a lawyer."

"Have you spoken with Giosuè about Alden?"

"You no longer need to worry about him," Bosco replied.

I gasped. "What does that mean?"

"He's fine, but if you want Giosuè to calm down, then I suggest not bringing up your ex."

"Giosuè is the one who barged his way into my life." I banged my palm on the top of the island.

"All I can say is that my brother doesn't go around bringing anyone home to meet the family."

I lifted the spoon, stirring the tomato soup. "Thanks for letting me know I'm so lucky."

Bosco stepped from the counter and planted both hands on the top. "Relax since your professor is still alive."

I choked on the soup at his comment. "Professor Williams? Please, tell me no harm has come to him. It was my idea to try to escape."

"Finish your soup. I think Giosuè will come around over time." Bosco exited the kitchen, leaving Maggie and me alone.

Maggie patted my hand. "He cares about you."

"Maggie, how can you work for a man so evil?" I dropped my spoon in the bowl and threw my hands up.

"Mr. Calabresi is a great man; I promise you that he will never hurt you."

"Hard to believe."

"The professor sent your schoolwork—and here's a video of Aspen and Lucy together, going to see Alden in the hospital." Maggie held up a video from her cell, handing it to me.

"How did you get this?"

"Giosuè has video from the hospital."

I flicked through the recording, seeing my best friends hugging Alden and dropping off flowers. I closed out of the video, and another one popped up of Aspen and me. I clicked on the video of us going in the café near the school, then my condo.

I raised my head in shock. "He has a video of my condo?"

"He does."

"Why?" Maggie was sweet, but it was hard to disguise my annoyance in her presence.

"Giosuè is complicated."

I shoved the phone at her. "He's a stalker and killer." I headed out of the kitchen and stomped down the entryway to his office. I extended my hand to knock when I heard whispers coming from two male voices.

"No matter how long you stand there, you won't be able to hear anything."

I jumped at the voice behind me, turning to see Armani with both hands shoved in his pockets.

"Look, we both know I shouldn't be here."

He gave a blank look and chucked his head up in agreement. "True."

"So, talk to him and convince him that I won't say anything. I just want my old life back."

"Too late."

"Why? I promise not to speak about what happened to Alden. My professor will keep quiet."

"Once you've crossed the Calabresi line of sight, you become insulated. Unfortunately, you aren't my first choice, but my brother is the boss, and what he says is signed as law."

It would be entertaining to be in a back and forth with him, but Armani literally is the epitome of arrogant and smug. "So, you're his puppet?"

Armani smirked, pulled his hand up to his chin, and brushed across his beard. "I am the one they call to make things go poof in the night." He circled around me, then entered his brother's office.

"Miss Hutton, I have the rest of your food ready." A housekeeper stopped and motioned toward the dining room. I sauntered in to sit down.

"Can I use the telephone?"

"Ma'am, I am not allowed."

"What's your name?"

She kept her eyes down. "Lisa."

"Lisa, how long have you been here?"

"Mr. Calabresi saved my life. I won't betray him." Lisa started to rush off, and I reached for her hand.

"Wait, Lisa, please. I need to check in on my friend."

"Lisa, go take care of the dinner menu." Maggie arrived and dismissed her. The entire staff kept his secrets; he probably threatened their families to get what he wanted. Maggie went back to the kitchen, leaving me to eat alone.

I dropped my fork and rose from my chair. I shifted to the window and stared out at the acres of land, featuring a guest house, pool, and jacuzzi. Rarely did I have the chance to live in a place that held unlimited luxuries, yet for some reason Giosuè wanted to place it all at my feet. Should I have been disgusted or flattered?

"It's unlocked."

I swiveled around at his deep voice. "I see no reason to go out there."

"I hadn't gotten word Lucinda was the one who came after you today."

"So that means?"

"That means you will continue to be under my protection. I'm still waiting for confirmation. I never put anything past Lucinda."

"Protection or for pleasure? I mean, I do escort."

That statement got to him if his harsh frown was any indication. He strode out of the room without answering my question. Maybe me pushing his buttons would force him to realize I wouldn't go with the flow of his little kidnapping.

I sighed, faced the backyard, and tapped my hand on the window. I watched his staff clean the pool and talk to each other, like I was someone who wasn't being held captive. While I preoccupied myself, I sat back at the table and reached for my glass, gulped down the iced tea, and filled my stomach. After cleaning up my food, I grabbed the dishes and carried them back to the kitchen, piled them in the sink, and started washing them.

Lisa and Maggie popped back in.

"Oh, Penelope, you don't need to clean up, dear."

"Sorry, it's a habit of mine. Growing up with my grandmother I was in charge of cleaning the dishes and she cooked."

Maggie smiled, lifting a towel and wiggling her hand for me to pass the dishes to her to dry. Lisa wrapped up the leftover food and placed it in the fridge. I finished the last plate, wiped my hands on the paper towel, and pressed my back to the counter.

"I tried to run away, and Giosuè had my ex-boyfriend shot," I announced, rocking on my feet.

Maggie and Lisa both froze in place, glancing at me then each other.

"Penelope." Maggie slipped off her gloves and waved at Lisa to exit the kitchen.

"Can you assure me that he's not dangerous?"

Maggie clamped her hands together. "He has methods I do not agree with—"

I snickered. "Yeah, well his methods are insane. Obviously you agree since you work for him." I shook my head and strode to my bedroom.

Chapter 7

Giosuè

Every plan I had ran smoothly and the moment my obsession with Penelope Hutton came into my head, nothing else mattered. Bosco held the stacks of cash in the center of the table next to the last haul of product that Matevi ran from the ports and the garbage pickups. The decision to work alongside him became profitable, but with the shooting I was apprehensive of continuing. Bosco and Armani were handling the new pickup when they got the call about Penelope trying to escape from her class. At first, I wanted to kill Macsen for letting her slip out of his sight, giving in to her wanting to leave the room. Since I couldn't finish my scheduled business, I left to find her and saw her ex-boyfriend in the car with her. The picture alone burned in my brain and I hoped it ended with his death, but that would be too cruel on my part. Penelope would realize she was mine and only belonged to me. I watched Bosco run down the next shipment coming tonight, and if we needed to have extra men on standby.

"Put at least another three or four around the area."

"I guess that means we'll feel a little safer with that

amount." Elio, my younger cousin from Chicago, smirked and swaggered in like he called the shots.

I rose from my chair and put my hand out to shake. "When did you get here? I had plans to meet you at the hotel."

Elio went around shaking up with Bosco and Armani, while the other crew stood off to the side. My family hadn't visited in a long time and to see him now married with a wife... my other cousins that have kids made me proud to see the Calabresi live on forever.

"You should have called. We could have picked you up from the airport."

Elio loosened the button on his jacket and sat down. "I had some things to handle. How is business?"

"Business is good, bigger things are happening."

"I heard you took a woman." Elio grinned, propped his feet up on the table.

I glared at Armani. "I wonder where you got that idea."

"Cousin, I understand about finding a woman that drives you crazy enough to kidnap her," Elio chuckled, along with my brothers.

I grunted and flipped my tie from my suit jacket. "She was in danger."

Elio pointed at me. "Danger from you or someone else?"

"I asked you over the phone. I want her to get an internship." We observed as Bosco ran more money through the counter, wrapped it into smaller bills, and bagged it up in a suitcase.

"From what you said she's doing family law," Elio remarked.

"I think getting her feet wet working in corporate law will be a good start."

"When is she finished with school?"

Bosco packed up another suitcase and slid it to a few soldiers to load onto the truck.

"In a few months."

Elio straightened up in his armchair. "I'd like to talk to her first. I know she has to be smart, but as a businessman, I need to make sure the right people are in place."

"Understood. How is your wife doing?"

"Amazing, still working as usual. Entire family wants you all to visit."

"We'll need to make that happen."

"And the business with the Russians?" Elio relaxed in the chair and clasped hands.

"Matevi is on a test run with garage pickups, but I might cut it short if he had involvement with the gallery shooting."

"He might be on his own, but you know very well that could be a lie."

"In due time we will discover the truth."

Armani motioned to his team to help grab more stacks of the crates filled with guns to ship out.

"Like Savio, we try to stay out of your business dealings, but cousin, keep your eyes open. Easy money is never less complicated." Elio confirmed my thoughts.

"Bosco, what did your research show on him?"

"Matevi had everything on time. We made twenty million from the deal. So far, I have no complaints." Bosco became distracted by his phone ringing.

Elio suggested, "Up the next drop as a test."

"What about Lucinda?" Armani inquired.

"Have you found her yet?" I investigated.

"Still searching. The house was empty when we searched and even her little boy toy bodyguard hasn't been seen around town," Armani explained.

"Look harder. Has her ex left the hospital?"

Armani drew the clipboard of the orders from the wall. "Yes. Do you want us to talk with him? His family had some security around his apartment, but I can get around that."

"I want you to stay on him—in case he tries to contact her."

Armani finished writing on the document. "I will."

"Are you going to kill him?" Elio probed.

I grinned and rose from the seat. "Let's go talk to him and see If I need to make that happen."

Armani, Bosco, and Elio all trailed me out of the basement, leaving the Calabresi building. Macsen drove us to the apartment Alden's parents rented for him, parking on street. I got out of the limo, and Armani followed, checking his gun. I waved it off. Alden was not a threat to me. I lifted my palm to knock, waiting for an answer when I heard a TV playing in the background. The locks turned, and Alden appeared, disheveled, like he'd been asleep. He was wearing an arm sling.

"Alden Katz."

He rubbed his eyes into focus. "Yeah, who are you?"

"Penelope's husband."

He chuckled at my words. "Penelope's not married."

I pushed him back and moved around him to walk into an apartment that hadn't been cleaned in a week or two. "She's not a concern for you. I came here to make it known you will no longer have contact."

Alden's cheeks grew hot. "No one invited you inside my place." He fidgeted with his hands, taken a back at the amount of people with me.

"Looks like you need to realize who you're dealing with, Mr. Katz."

Alden retreated and threw his hands up. "Penelope and I broke up a long time ago."

I formed my finger into a gun and pretended to shoot at him. "I know, so take my words like the threat they're meant to be. If you come within five feet of Penelope, the next gunshot will be to your head."

His eyes drifted to Armani. "I will stay away."

"Not just staying away. She no longer exists to you."

"Yea-aah," he stuttered,

"Clean up this filthy apartment and stop wasting Arthur and Sally's monthly rent." I slapped him on the arm, then left his place.

Macsen started up the vehicle and drove away from the apartment, as I listened to Elio and Bosco joke about my obsession with Penelope.

"He probably pissed himself when you threatened to kill him," Armani voiced, securing his seatbelt.

I drew out my phone and logged into the camera on Penelope. "Fuck him."

"Penelope will hate you even more," Bosco laughed.

Gesturing to the phone in my hand, Elio suggested, "To get her on your side, you need to be less threatening."

"Is that how you got your woman to come back to you? I recall you forced a visit to New York." I brought up his last visit when his ex didn't want anything to do with him, and he took her and flew her across the country.

"We're talking about you," Elio teased.

I pressed the button to roll down the partition. "Macsen, take us to Lucinda's."

"What are you planning on doing?" Elio wondered.

I dumped the cell next to me on the seat. "Have a little fun."

"Are you sure you want to find her this way?" Bosco remarked.

I removed the lighter from my pocket, smirking at the next move that would bring Lucinda to the forefront.

Thirty minutes passed before Macsen made the stop at Lucinda's whorehouse, which had sat empty for a few days. Right after the shooting, Lucinda must have known that we'd think it was her, and she moved all the girls out.

After he parked, I shoved open the door, and my brothers followed my lead. "Grab the canister."

Armani waited for Macsen to unlock the trunk, then started to remove lighter fluid and canisters from what we needed.

Bosco jogged up to the house and checked the lock. It was open. We stepped into an empty space, with the furniture still sitting in place.

"She probably planned on coming back," Armani stated, walked around the living room, back to hallway.

I bent down and snatched a few pieces of mail that were addressed to Lucinda. "Burn it down."

A mask of reserve covered Bosco's face. "That's not a good look."

Armani started pouring the gasoline around the room. Elio talked on the phone, laughing with his brothers. "He's crazy over some girl, I haven't met her yet."

I dumped the mail back on the floor. "I remember you doing some crazy shit."

"At least my girl liked me," Elio snapped and disconnected his call.

I flipped him off and brought the flame up ready to burn the house down. "Go outside and wait."

"Either Lucinda will make contact or she will see this as an act of war," Armani said.

"Then let the battle begin."

I dropped the canister inside and the flames rose high.

Everybody backed out of the home and watched from the street as the fire tore through the mansion. The neighbors lived a few miles away, so the emergency trucks would take a while to arrive.

After giving Armani a ride to his condo, Bosco and Elio rode home with me. Macsen parked, and I slid out of the backseat. My butler, Abel, let us in and waited for me to remove my coat and gloves for him to put away.

"Is she up?"

"She is, sir," Abel responded.

"Elio follow me."

"She's in the theater room," Abel told me.

Bosco went to the kitchen, and Elio came up behind me to the theater off the hallway staircase. I heard the loudspeakers playing and reached for the sliding door. Penelope sat and rotated her head toward me. For her to have gotten so comfortable and still hate to be locked up brought amusement to me. Being cynical was my normal attitude with people who tried to test my authority, but for her, I would let go, depending on her next statement. "Can we talk?"

"Do you have any plans to let me go?"

Elio chuckled and I forced out a loud sigh.

I lifted the remote and paused the movie. "I checked with Alden and he's fine."

Penelope glanced from me to Elio.

I settled down on the loveseat next to her. "Elio Calabresi, my cousin."

"Hello." Penelope placed her bowl of popcorn on the seat and folded her arms.

Elio held a hand up to wave. "Nice to meet you, Penelope."

"Are you crazy like your cousin?" Penelope asked.

"Not as bad," Elio answered, laughing and shaking his head.

"Elio has connections to get you an internship."

Penelope's a woman of natural mysteries and defiance. She had Lucinda fooled, but I could see the sparkle in her eye. She liked the chase. "So, you can clear your conscience."

"My conscience will forever be clear, baby. I'm a man of many things, but compassion is never in my thoughts."

"Is killing people your job or something?"

I shrugged, sat back, stretched my arm behind the back of the couch, and tugged on her ponytail. "Making money is my therapy."

Penelope slapped my hand and scooted away. "Thank you for the opportunity, Elio, but I decline."

I ignored her and glanced at my cousin. "She's going to take it, Elio."

Penelope jumped up in a huff. "I can speak for myself. I don't want anything to do with you." She paced back and forth.

"Penelope, my cousin is slightly demanding. My family has told him many times to be a little softer." Elio walked up to Penelope and clasped a hand on her shoulder.

I glared at Elio.

He headed to the bar and grabbed a glass, pouring some bourbon. "Penelope, you're a bright girl. I saw your school records."

Penelope buried her face in her hands and groaned. "Has he told you that my professor is going to flunk me after I skipped out on his class."

"All right, I will compromise on one condition." I hated for her to carry on a full conversation with my cousin, like he was the only one she could depend on. The mere touch of his fingers on her shoulder pissed me off.

Penelope moved backwards, hands on her hip. "What's the catch?" I finally noticed the little boy shorts and thin t-shirt she wore with long snoopy socks.

"My men will be around the clock watching you."

"Fine, and my friends? Can I see them now? Lucinda or whoever has probably forgotten about me."

"She's right," Elio said.

My pissed off reaction seemed to amuse him. "No one asked you. All right—if you promise not to run again, then I can promise on letting you go out."

Elio extended a glass filled with bourbon to Penelope and she waved it off and sat back down.

Penelope pulled her feet underneath her legs. "Thank you."

Elio handed me the drink instead.

"Alden is off limits. Boys have a natural instinct when they lose the best girl they ever had—and Alden would be a fool to not try to make contact again. I will have my men make him disappear for real."

"Alden is my ex."

"I know and we've spoken."

She reached for the popcorn and tossed some in her mouth. "What did you do?"

"After he tried to help you escape, I had a few words so were on the same page."

"You're crazy."

"Crazy for you."

Bosco appeared with a frown on his face. I hopped up and met him halfway.

"What's wrong?"

Bosco backed away and motioned to come in the hall-way. "We got a problem."

I gazed at Penelope and back to Elio, then Bosco. "Let's talk in my office."

Elio followed us, closed the door, and took a seat on the couch. Bosco brushed a hand down his face. Bosco huffed and marched to the bathroom, turned on the faucet, and washed his face.

"Matevi never showed up."

I stood at the door and watched him dry his hands and face. "How do you know?"

"He knows the check in point and his partner said he called out sick," Bosco explained.

"Who all knew about your deal?" Elio checked.

Bosco extended his phone to show the location pickup. "Only us and Matevi—plus his partner."

"Any idea if his partner would kill him?" Elio questioned, making me think.

"Matevi was in charge of the entire deal. His partner in the truck only knew about the specific path, but not what they had to pick up," Bosco replied.

"Bosco, mistakes should not be happening."

My office line rang, interrupting the conversation. I grabbed the landline to answer, sat at my desk, and typed on the desktop to pull up the directions. "Hello."

"Mr. Calabresi."

"Who is this?" I motioned for Elio to sit closer.

The Russian voice spoke directly. "Very interesting how you do business."

I waved to Bosco to trace the number with our tech team. Elio sat up straight, and I pressed the button to put the phone on speaker.

"How much longer did you and your family feel we

would let you run without cutting us in on the deal?" he asked.

Bosco leaned on the desk and picked up a pen and paper. *Keep talking*, he wrote.

"Where's Matevi?" I commanded, yanking my tie loose.

"In a place you can visit if we aren't on the same page."

I bit the inside of my jaw. "Motherfucker."

"Losing your cool..." The taunting pissed me off. "The ports and drops will be made fully to me moving forward."

I logged into our camera footage from the ports and office buildings. "And if we don't"

"Common policy says family and loved ones can come up missing."

Bosco stretched his hand out, showing that he had something. "No deal." I placed the phone back on the receiver and sat up in the chair, staring off through the window. I reared my head back. "Who are we dealing with?"

"The number is traced back to a Bulgarian area code." Bosco read from his phone, then flipped it around to show me.

"The Bulgarians stepping into our territory is not good."

"Have they tried to work with you before? You know we've had issues in the past," Elio reminded us.

"Matevi must have told them about the deal."

"Never got a chance to really make money," Bosco said.

I sighed, raking a hand on the back of my neck. "I hate to kill an entire family and it make it back to some of our friends."

Elio picked up the phone and dialed. "Let me make some calls."

"I promised Penelope that I would let her go out. I will look stupid if she's locked back up."

"For now, keep it normal. Obviously, they have no clue about Penelope." Bosco planted a hand on my shoulder and squeezed.

I started to get up to walk him out. "Are you leaving?"

"Yeah, Armani needs a heads up. Triple up our security." Bosco strolled away. I eased back in the armchair, stared at the phone, and clasped my hands together in thought.

"Must be difficult to have everyone's life in your hands." Penelope startled me.

"You're talking to me."

Penelope stood at the entryway. "I have no choice; everyone here is too scared to carry on a conversation."

I got back up and walked around, getting a few feet closer to Penelope.

"Miss Hutton, I have your clothes sorted." Maggie stuck her head into my office, and Penelope looked at her and smiled, then walked over to leave.

"Mr. Calabresi, are you hungry?" Maggie questioned.

"Save it for later. I have some calls to make."

Maggie and Penelope left me alone, the calmness from the brief talk kept the monster hidden. Only time would tell me if she could handle the real me.

I sat on the edge and dialed the number that Bosco had for Matevi. It rang a few times, and then went to voicemail.

The sound of a text message on my phone took up my attention. I checked the thread, seeing an unknown number.

Unknown: *Fire was a nice choice.*
Me: *Lucinda?*
Unknown: *Sounds like you've made more enemies than friends.*
Me: *Lucinda, meet up with me, and I might not kill you.*

Unknown: *Your precious Penelope won't be yours for long.*
Me: *Try a different approach.*
Unknown: *Money to replace what you've destroyed.*
Me: *I already made you a fair offer.*
Unknown: *Not enough!*
Me: *I will burn more than your house down Lucinda.*
Unknown: *This is not Lucinda.*
Me: *Play big boy games with me, then show your face. Let's meet in person.*
Unknown: *Nice try.*
Me: *Fuck you.*
Unknown: *I will do that soon enough with your bitch.*

I shoved the phone in my pocket and went to check on Penelope and saw her holding up a dress wearing only shorts and bra. I eased from her room before she noticed and walked to my bedroom to shower and head to bed.

Chapter 8

Penelope

"We have breaking news that Heath Laurier officially has enough funds to secure more ads and scheduled his next fundraiser for his campaign to Congress." Channel Four News ran the report. I sat in the café, waiting for Aspen and Lucy to meet me for lunch. The sky was clear, and the streets were filled with crowds. A couple of days ago, Giosuè agreed to let me back on campus as long as Macsen and a few other men monitored me. At first, I felt it was overzealous, but I wouldn't try to run off anymore. Their cousin, Elio, would have me starting an internship soon, and I was kind of excited to be moving in that direction.

Macsen, Banner, and two other men who didn't speak spread out to give me some privacy. The door swung open, and Aspen ran in with her arms waving high. "Penelope!"

We held onto each other tight. "Aspen, Lucy, so glad you came." I released them both, motioning to the menu to order some food.

"You had us stressed," Lucy sassed as she put her purse on the table.

"Sorry, my life has gone from busy to crazy differ-ent." I scanned the café. Seeing Macsen's closed body posture was a telltale sign to keep certain stuff to myself.

"Who is he?" Lucy questioned.

I elevated my palm to rub my forehead. "Um."

"Did you hear about Alden?" Aspen checked, popping bubbles with the gum in her mouth.

"Guys... I need a drink and then I will explain every-thing," I whispered softly and sat forward, keeping eye contact.

In response, Lucy extended a hand over the table to mine.

They had a QR-code sticker on the table. Aspen took out her phone and scanned it.

"We're here for you, babe." Lucy's courage and encour-agement were like a breath of fresh air.

"Thank you. It's crazy to even talk about." I glanced around the café, making sure that Giosuè's people weren't listening to the conversation.

Aspen placed her phone down. "You are shaking. What happened? Be honest, Penelope."

The waitress shuffled to our table. "Miss Hutton, you have a call." The waitress held up a cell with an unknown number.

Hesitantly, I grabbed the phone. "H-Hello," I stam-mered. As the waitress stood off to the side, another wait-staff brought our drinks.

"For our deal to work, we can't have you telling any of our business," Giosuè expressed.

In shock, I reared back and pulled the phone from my ear. "What—"

"Penelope, please understand that if you spill any

details, it will put your friends in danger." He waited, challenging me to go through with it.

It was as if my throat was tightening at Aspen and Lucy being put in a bad situation because of me. "I understand."

Giosuè said, "Glad we can come to a compromise. Enjoy your lunch."

Right when I finished the waitress set down our plates. I gave the phone back and slowly picked up the glass of water to take a gulp.

Aspen tapped the top of the table. "Penelope, you're scaring us." She searched anxiously for any answers.

"How is Alden doing?"

"He's fine now. His parents want him to take some time off." Lucy dispensed ketchup on her fries.

I blurted out quietly, "I was there when he got shot."

Both of them stopped eating with their mouth agape.

"Are you saying you shot him? I mean, you two broke up a long time ago." Lucy's brow crinkled in confusion.

While waving my hand and whispering, I urged her to keep quiet. "Lucy, I did not shoot him."

A few people stared at our section. I cleared my voice and took a piece of my chicken salad sandwich. Macsen stood at the front entrance, watching us and making me rethink even coming to lunch in the first place.

"All I can say is that I am fine. I've been sick for a little while."

Aspen nudged Lucy in the arm. "Something tells me you're keeping secrets."

The guards weren't paying attention to me, and I felt I had the perfect moment.

I stretched my hand toward her. "Can I see your phone?"

"Sure, who are you calling? Have you heard the news

about Lucinda's place catching on fire?" Aspen finished the rest of her sandwich.

Panic like never before welled in my throat. "On fire?"

"It was all on the news, the police and fire department had the area blocked off from people going and taking pictures," Aspen informed me.

"She tried to kill me," I whispered to myself. Fear coated my eyes.

"Wait! Why are you just telling us now? Unless you got payback with the fire?" Lucy's eyes sparkled devilishly.

I yanked Aspen and Lucy's hands into mine. "I need help."

Although Aspen tried to remain calm, the disturbance in her posture at my erratic behavior sent her signals. "Okay."

"Some people are watching me, like bodyguards who don't look away, because of Lucinda and they think she's going to try again soon."

"Then we need to go to the police." Aspen worried, taking both my hands in hers.

"The police might arrest me. Being an escort is not doing me any favors, plus being one of Lucinda's girls will draw too much attention."

"How can we help?" Lucy inquired.

"Research what you can about Calabresi family."

Lucy and Aspen stared, then spoke at the same time. "The cartel."

"You've heard of them?"

"What planet are you living on that you've never heard of the Calabresi cartel family? Any of their enemies—and sometimes, even their friends—will go missing." Lucy swallowed the despair in her throat.

"Keep your voices down. I already said too much."

Aspen hopped out of her chair. "Are they listening in on us? Oh my god. Penelope, what the hell have you done."

I tugged her by the arm before Macsen could come over and check on us. "Sit down!"

Lucy scanned the room. "Penelope, we're here to help, but you need to be honest."

"Yeah, I agree with Lucy. I am too young to get caught in some mob hits." Aspen frowned in aggravation.

"All I know is that Lucinda and Calabresi are in some war."

Waitstaff came back to the table to take our empty plates. "Would you like anything else?"

I smiled, reached in my purse to remove my wallet, and shook my head. "No, leave the check."

"Here you go." She left the bill on the table.

I scooted back from the table, sickened at what my life had become. "I have to get back into school."

Aspen grasped my arm, stopping me from walking away. "They're forcing you from school?"

I stretched my arm around her for a hug. "Nothing I tell you can get back to your families. I shouldn't have told you this much."

"Promise." Lucy crossed her heart.

"I told Lucinda I would be leaving and focusing more on my studies. With me graduating, I had no reason to keep escorting. Well, she took it hard and threatened me. Somehow, Calabresi found out and told me she tried to kill me." I released all the secrets I held, feeling a weight being lifted from my shoulders.

"The only way they would know about Lucinda is if they were in the escort business," Aspen remarked.

"Giosuè said she's into human trafficking. Apparently

about to sell me overseas before they brought me here." Once I finished signing the bill, I started to leave. Lucy and Aspen left money for a tip and walked with me to the entrance. Macsen scanned outside, going out front.

"My goal is to get my school papers finished so I can graduate on time."

Lucy pointed at Macsen, who was standing by the limo. "Is he your bodyguard or something?"

"The—" I started to respond.

"Hey, Penelope." A guy I'd never seen before came up to me. I took a step back and he grasped my arm, yanking me to him.

"Let her go!" Lucy and Aspen screamed at the same time.

Macsen jogged over as I pushed out of the man's tight grip.

"Penelope!" A loud shot went off, everybody ducked down, and I scrambled to cover myself, feeling a large body on top of me.

Macsen gently cupped my chin. "Penelope, hold on."

I checked around to find Aspen and Lucy safe near other guards, Macsen rolled the dead body off me, then grabbed my arm to help me stand.

"Are you hit?" Macsen turned me from left to right.

"No, I'm fine." Slowly I felt around my arm, legs, and chest for any wounds.

Macsen turned me so I didn't face the guy on the ground. "We need to get you home."

I wiped sweat off my forehead with a shaking hand. My heart rate increased at the sight of the blood. "What about him?" It was hard to fight back my emotions. I'd never had to deal with someone being killed in my presence.

Banner held a cell up to his ear. "Our people will clean it up."

"Aspen and Lucy, come with me."

"No, Mr. Calabresi won't like visitors," Macsen said. His conflicted stare with Banner showed they hated to go along with me.

"Macsen, either they come with me or I am going to scream."

He sighed and whipped out his phone to make a call. I figured he was checking with Giosuè about letting them come to his home. Either way I had no problem with making a scene and with police sirens coming closer that meant questions they would not be ready to answer.

Macsen turned on his heel and strode to the car. "He said to drop them off at home."

"Let me—"

"Miss Hutton, please, I am trying to do my job."

"Penelope, we'll be fine. Cops are coming and if we get in trouble, all of us will get arrested." Lucy leaned her head on Aspen's shoulder.

"She's right, Penelope." Aspen released breath.

Banner stalked to the limo, and I reached out to give them both a hug goodbye. "I will try to get in touch with you soon."

Aspen pressed a kiss on my cheek. "Be safe, Penelope."

I watched as Lucy climbed in Aspen's Jeep, then turned into traffic to get distance from the scene. I ducked down and climbed in the car, clicked the seatbelt, and rubbed up and down my arms to keep my anxiety under control.

* * *

Early Monday morning after I got dressed, I slammed the bedroom door in frustration. Giosuè had promised to let me have more freedom. Since I'd had lunch with my friends, Giosuè had avoided me and had his staff give me the runaround about his whereabouts. Today, I planned on making it known that I was here because of the egos of two people who hated to lose. I marched down the hall and knocked on his bedroom door. I had seen Maggie come and go from this direction. I assumed it was Giosuè's bedroom, and I started to raise my fist up high to bang again when it yanked open.

"Ahhhh!"

He jerked me inside and pushed me up against the wall, wearing a towel around his waist. Water dripped down the six pack of muscles and his wide shoulders and thick arms. I knew he was older than me, and the darkness in his eyes told me I shouldn't press his buttons further.

Giosuè grunted and tugged on my loose hair. "I hate noise."

I opened my mouth to say something, but he stopped me with his hand in the air.

"Before you say anything that pisses me off, understand I will put you over my knee."

In confusion, I hesitated, blinking. "Spank me?"

He smirked, caressing my chin. "Spank you for disobeying my rules."

"Rules that shouldn't even apply to me. My friends could have died yesterday." I reached my hands to his shoulders to try to shove him back.

Giosuè stepped back to put distance between us and walked to his bed to grab his clothes. Right in front of me, he started loosening his towel. It fell to the ground, and I saw the tight muscles that traveled from his chest, down to his legs, and then to a dick that had girth and length. It twitched.

I pivoted away to cover my eyes. "Oh, shit." Ironic I was embarrassed of a naked body, even though I worked as an escort.

Giosuè teased, "We're grown, Penelope."

"I have to go." I angled around to catch the doorknob.

"Macsen's job is to keep you safe, especially with enemies running around to get to me."

"I'm nothing to you, Giosuè," I said with my back to him.

"Macsen will take you to class. If I discover you've taken off again, then it won't be pretty, Little Dove."

I spun to face him. "After being locked up, I doubt you can do any worse." I held my head up high. We had a stare-off—until he smirked.

Giosuè's tongue sprang out and went over his lips. "Try me."

I marched back to my room, picked up my bookbag and jacket, and left to go downstairs. I caught Macsen talking with a few other men.

"Ready to head out."

"Mr. Calabresi stated you will only be going to class and back here," Macsen said in a tense, clipped voice that forbade any questions.

"Fun." I grinned, stomping out of the house and hearing the whispers behind me. If Giosuè thought that I would sit still and not try to get away again, then he should have chained me to the bed. Even without a phone, getting in touch with my girls shouldn't be too hard.

Once I made it to school, Macsen, Banner, and the rest of the men trailed me into the building. I sat in the back listening to Professor Williams explain the essay that's due in two weeks. The library was my next stop, and I hoped it would give me a bit of relief from my guards. Everyone started to pick up their stuff to go, and a few people asked me why I was absent. I lied about my family being sick.

Becky was one of the quiet girls I'd met in my freshmen year. She asked, "So, Penelope, will you come?"

"Come?"

"The end of the year party they're throwing at Morgan Hall," Becky pressed, making me regret even talking to her in the first place. Macsen barely gave us any wiggle room.

I broke past him with my open hand. "Probably not, Becky. Too much work to catch up on."

"Well, if you change your mind, then Aspen and Lucy already made plans to help set up."

"Setup committee? What day and time?"

Becky laid her books on the table in the rear.

"Tomorrow around three at my dorm. Only have two classes so it makes it easy."

"I'd love to help. Do you have your phone?"

Becky lent me her cell and I typed in my number, then texted Aspen.

Me: *Are you on campus? It's Penelope.*
Aspen: *Penelope, what are you doing? Whose phone are you using?*
Me: *No time for questions, I need your help.*
Aspen: *I'm here in the cafeteria.*
Me: *Great, meet me in the library.*
Aspen: *On my way.*
Me: *Leave Lucy out of it and come to the side near the exit and bathroom.*
Aspen: *I'm nervous. What's going on, Penelope?*
Me: *Taking a chance to get out of here.*

Aspen: *And school?*
Me: *I can start over somewhere else.*

"Is everything okay?" Becky checked.

I looked up, moved out of the message thread, and picked up my notebook. "Actually, I need your help, Becky. Do you mind if I hold onto your phone?"

Becky flipped through her books. "I guess."

"I need to run to the restroom. Can you pick out the books we need?" I lowered my voice to not cause alarm as Macsen continued watching me. I shifted to the hallway, and Macsen traced my steps . I glanced over my shoulder like I was fine.

I pointed at the signs on the walls. "Restroom."

"No funny business, Miss Hutton."

"Macsen, you stressed?"

Macsen shook his head and ran a hand through his waves.

A woman walked out of the bathroom, holding the door open. I stepped in and held it open for Macsen to look inside. "Want a peek?"

Macsen placed a hand on the wall. "Please hurry, Miss Hutton."

"Suit yourself."

I rushed to shut the door, pushed open each stall, and paced back and forth waiting for Aspen to come. I felt my stomach shrink in on itself. My hands were sweaty at the thought of trying to run away again and keep my friends from getting hurt. A few second went by and the door flung wide with Aspen holding her purse and book bag in her hand.

"Penelope, there're men outside." Aspen's footsteps

shuffled in nervousness. Her energy left her in misery and anguish.

I wagged my hands in her face. "Shush, keep your voice down."

"That's hard to do when we already had a shooting," Aspen snapped.

I gripped her by the shoulders to calm her down and face me. "He's not letting me out of his sight. I need your help."

Her hand went to her chest to control her breathing. "How? Maybe you can call the police. My god, this is crazy."

"Not yet. I want you to give me your keys and fake like you're sick."

"What do you intend to do?" The last traces of resistance vanished.

"The less you know the better."

"Is he planning to kill me?" A hot tear rolled down her cheek.

"No, because you're going to have too many eyes on you. Look, I won't be gone long. I need to talk to Heath."

"Why?"

"He's the only one that can contact Lucinda and get her to let me go."

Aspen's eyes blinked rapidly. "I'm worried about you, Penelope."

I cupped her hands. "I promise the faster I can get whatever deal squashed the better."

Aspen bundled me into her arms. "Okay."

I kissed both her hands as someone started to come in. I nudged Aspen downwards and sprinted to the wall, pulling the fire alarm.

"Ohhh, please call an ambulance."

Aspen whimpered, holding her stomach.

"Help! Someone, call 911!" a girl screamed.

Macsen flew in and shoved her to the side.

I bent down and held Aspen's hand. "Aspen, hold on. You're going to be all right. Help is on the way."

"What happened to her?" Macsen held the back of his palm against her forehead.

"We were talking and all of a sudden she complained about stomach issues."

"Penelope, I need you to step away," Macsen insisted and I threw a hand in the air.

"No! She's my best friend," I snapped, jerking my elbow out of his hold. The librarian helped the EMTs come in, and they started to question Aspen. I stood to the side while they talked with her, after a few moments they placed her on the stretcher, came out, and piled in the ambulance.

Macsen talked to his guards as I slowly moved from the back of the emergency transport to the right. I jogged to Aspen's Jeep parked near the student parking.

"Where is she?!"

I heard a boisterous voice.

"Macsen," I muttered and climbed in the Jeep. I backed out and sank down in the seat as I drove away from the school, holding onto Becky's phone.

"I need to get to Heath," I whispered, taking another turn before I could calm down and relax. I looked out the rear window to see if Macsen was following.

I dialed Heath's number. "Come on answer, god damn it."

An automatic voicemail came on and I hung up and attempted to call again.

"The hotel," I whispered, thinking of where I might find him.

Heath usually had meetings during the day and his campaign office was near Manhattan. I tried to dial his private number again when it was picked up.

"How do you have this number?" Heath demanded.

"It's me."

"Penelope."

"I need to see you."

Chapter 9

Giosuè

"Mr. Calabresi, we have the information you wanted."

"What do you know?" The car was silent as we drove to a meeting to talk with the Bulgarian Mafia leader, Paraskeva Abadjiev. Bosco secured some information from his contacts in Interpol, and we knew that doing business with Matevi might come back on us.

Sherman handed the folder to me. I scanned the pictures and call logs of Lucinda and Abadjiev going back and forth and making plans to do business.

I cocked my head to stretch. "Lucinda's working with him."

Sherman, a long-time computer hacker, pulled a cigarette out of his pocket.

"They're moving into your territory if you continue your pursuant."

"Lucinda's foolish." I closed the folder in my lap and tossed it onto the seat.

The loud buzzing of my phone distracted me. I saw Macsen's name, making me answer immediately. "Macsen."

There was a noticeable lack of breath coming from Macsen. "Boss."

"Where is she?" I had a hunch that she'd tried to escape again, so there was no reason to prolong the conversation.

"I don't know, sir."

Macsen had worked on my team for a long time, and he knew that I never gave second chances. Now I would have to explain to his family how he died tragically.

"She went to the bathroom."

"How many times did I say to go in the bathroom with her?"

"Sir."

"Shut the fuck up! Send me your location." I shouted, slamming my fist on the window.

I flung the folder to Sherman and brushed a hand down my face. "Head back to the city."

"Abadjiev doesn't like being stood up," Sherman pressed, fidgeting with putting the papers back in the folder.

I balled my fists. "Rearrange for another time. Something more important came up."

Penelope felt like playing games, so I would show her the way I ran my carnival, only no one would get satisfaction but me. Arriving at the hospital close to the school, Banner stood at the entry of her room, with his arms locked.

"Where's Macsen? Inside talking to the girl?"

"He's there and made sure no one is allowed in, not even the doctor, until you got here."

Banner eyed the nurse's station, exits, and elevators. I entered the room hearing Macsen's voice.

"Call her now," Macsen demanded.

Aspen whimpered and sank down onto her pillow. "I don't know where she's at."

I placed my hand above the food tray and lifted the cover. "Aspen." I moved closer to her bed.

Aspen titled her head back, swiping tears away. "Sorry, who are you?"

"Aspen, you really care about Penelope, correct?"

She crossed and uncrossed her hands, lips pressed in a thin line.

"As her best friend, you want to help her, I get it."

"Penelope never told me where she was going." Aspen gulped down the nervousness and labored breathing.

I adjusted my feet and moved my right hand to the IV bag. "Somehow, I believe you're lying."

"Mr. Calabresi." Aspen critically scanned my movements.

"Aspen, if you try to scream, then I will kill you. If you lie to me again, then I will kill you. Where is Penelope?" I gritted through my teeth.

"All she told me was that she needed to find Lucinda," Aspen blurted.

I removed my hand from my pocket. "Where is your phone?"

"Penelope kept it to call me," Aspen muttered.

I chucked my head at Macsen. "Track her."

Macsen marched out of the room, leaving us alone.

"Anything else you need to tell me?" I appraised her in the bed, falling apart.

Aspen's line of sight fell to her hands. "No—"

I tapped the IV bag, seeing the fear in her eyes. "Aspen, get well soon. Your family would have been hurt if something worse ended up happening."

Macsen ran in, out of breath. "Boss, she's with Heath."

"Heath Laurier." Her whereabouts sent a bad stench piercing my nose. She had run towards him for support.

"Boss, the phone tracked back to his office. I already sent a few men to grab her." Macsen's face carved into tormented lines at losing her again.

"No one touches her."

Macsen trailed beside me. "And Heath?"

I paused for a moment, feeling my pulse skyrocket, and hissed out a breath. "We can't touch him yet."

I directed Banner to stay with Aspen until she got discharged—just in case Penelope slipped away from Heath's and came back before I got there. The ride from the hospital normally took an hour, but busting through short cuts, we made it in half the time. Most of Heath's employees were out for lunch. I stalked down the hall to see Penelope sitting in the chair in front of his desk. Heath held her in his arms, turning my annoyance into rage. I extended my foot and kicked the door off the hinges, removed my gun, and pointed at his head. He squatted down.

Penelope jumped back. "Oh God!"

"Stand up." I narrowed my eyes at Heath, cocking the safety.

Penelope stood in front of him to block my view. "Please, Giosuè, listen to me."

I growled, "Penelope, I warned you."

Heath extended a hand to move Penelope behind him and I let off a shot close to his foot, making them both shrink in fear.

"Do you know who I am? I can have you arrested!" Heath yelled, grabbing Penelope's hand. I inclined my head to the side, winked at Penelope, and sent a shot above his head.

I gestured with my gun for Heath to get on the floor.

"Giosuè!" Penelope screamed.

"Stop playing with me or next it's going through his skull."

"Okay, nothing is going on between us. Heath is a client of Lucinda's. I thought I could get him to persuade her to leave me alone," Penelope pleaded.

I tucked the gun away. "Come on, let's go."

Penelope slowly stood with her head hung low. Heath stared at her back, while I moved to close the door inside his office and give us privacy.

"Do you think I give a shit that Penelope thinks you're a friend? Forget you've ever seen her face, or the campaign won't go in your favor."

"Lucinda has other girls. She's nothing to me," Heath said.

I strolled over to him lying on the floor and placed my foot over his palm, adding pressure.

Heath screamed, "Arghhh!"

"She's everything to me, and I never give second chances." I raked a hand down my jacket and left him on the floor in pain.

Penelope kept her gaze down on the ride back home. "Are you going to kill me?"

I turned her head to face me. "Heath Laurier is no client or friend to you Penelope."

Penelope glared at me. "Aspen—is she hurt?"

"Worry about yourself." I patted her leg, but she knocked my hand off.

"Don't touch me," Penelope snapped.

Macsen made it home in record time. Bosco's car was in the driveway, but I ignored it, took Penelope by the hand, and walked her around the outside of the house to another part of my home that I used for privacy.

"Where are we going?" Penelope tried to run away, and

I forced her up against the side of the brick wall, then gripped her by the chin to face me.

I set my leg firmly between her legs. Heat traveled in a slow wave at her sweet mouth in a full pout. "Be quiet."

"If you think I'm going to let you kill me quietly, then you're crazy." The landscape of her face held a host of emotions crisscrossing from hate to lust, defiance, and curiosity.

I caressed her left cheek with the back of my palm. "Keep fighting. I like it."

Her eyes grew wide. "You're insane."

"And you've pissed me off and now it's time to punish you."

She pressed one hand against my chest. I gripped them both and held them high above her head. "No! Let me go."

I bent down and lifted her body over my shoulder. I pulled the key out of my pocket and unlocked the door, stepped in, and set her down. I kept the lights turned off. The hallway led to one of my favorite playrooms I had built for when I would have someone, not necessarily a wife.

"Go open the door."

Penelope gazed over her shoulder. "Trying to lock me up again?"

"See for yourself." I stood to the side and let her canvass the king-sized bed with the black silk sheets, the gold-trimmed fireplace underneath the mounted TV, and the large paintings of naked women in different positions.

"Take off your clothes and go shower."

Her head swiveled around. "What will you do?"

"For disobeying me, I owe you ten spankings." I rolled up my sleeves, reached into the drawer, and pulled out a paddle. My playroom was built to give pleasure and pain. Penelope taking it upon herself to defy me again made me want to dominate her even more. Her feisty mouth would be filled with my come and balls in due time. I would keep her occupied with just me.

Penelope locked her hands on her hips. "Being an escort, I've seen it all. If you're trying to scare me, I'm not." She swiveled around and headed to the bathroom. The shower turned on. The steam from the bathroom wafted in the air. I trekked to the bar in the corner and released the top on a bottle of whiskey. I poured a shot and drank it quickly. Penelope stood in a towel, her wet hair covering just below her thick curves. "I have clothes for you."

Penelope swished her hips over to the bed and picked up the short silk lingerie set and thin top that I'd laid out for her. She turned to head back to the bathroom.

"Stop," I commanded.

She looked over her shoulder. "What?"

I gulped the next shot. It hit my throat, and I licked my lips. "Get dressed right here."

She squinted her eyes. "In front of you?"

Her defiance was exhilarating. The more push and pull building between us, the better it would be once I had her completely.

Her rich, warm rosy skin flushed under my stare.

"Am I supposed to be obedient once you spank me?" Her full lashes beat softly.

As soon as I closed the distance, her breath quickened, and she closed her eyes at the touch of my hand gliding down her cheek.

I leaned in to whisper, "Turn around, Penelope." I felt her body shiver at my touch trailing down her neck.

Appreciating her determination to push my buttons, I snaked a hand up her back, nudged her closer by the neck, rubbed a hand along waist, down to her thick ass and slapped it once.

"Ughhh..." Penelope moaned, tucking the clothes in her hands.

"Now since you refused to listen and put on the clothes, get on the bed."

She contemplated for a brief moment, then dropped the clothes on the floor and crawled on top of the bed.

I released the towel from her body, lifted the paddle to move it slowly around her ass, then positioned my body to the side of the bed.

"Have you been spanked before?"

"No." Slowly and seductively, her gaze slid down to my crotch.

"Have I made myself clear multiple times, Penelope?"

"Yes." Her answer was eager, the sound of her voice sent excitement through me.

Slap!

"So why are you constantly taking me as a fool?"

Slap!

"Ohhh..." Her emotions melted my resolve, but I willed myself to keep going.

I eased a hand in her hair, snatched it back, and growled in her ear. "I can't wait to fuck you."

"Giosuè," she cooed, lifting her eyes to me.

"Giving me those sweet eyes won't make the punishment less."

"I'm sorry."

Slap!

Penelope tried to touch my hand, but I moved out of her reach.

"Sorry for getting Aspen involved in my business? Do you understand you belong to me?"

Slap!

I released her hair, moved behind her, and bent down and kissed each ass cheek. My dick was straining to fuck her into submission. I had plans to handle business, and then take her to my place out of the city until the Bulgarians were killed. I can hear Armani yelling now about getting her out of our lives because she's caused nothing but problems.

Penelope spread her legs open. "Tell me the truth."

I rocked on my feet, amused by her anger at not getting the full treatment. "Get dressed we have somewhere to be."

"You're not going to force me to have sex?"

I planted both hands on the bed and glowered at her. "Forcing women? Baby, I'm a monster in certain things, but you will come to me on your own."

Penelope stood and hugged herself. The loud bell from the house intercom let me know my brothers were here.

I snatched up her clothes and handed them to her to get dressed. "Repeating myself will not happen again, Penelope. Aspen, Lucy, and Alden aren't your friends anymore."

The sadness appearing in her eyes told me she still wanted to run, but she nodded in agreement, slipped her legs in the shorts, and put on the thin silk shirt. I took her by the hand, and we walked into the main house. I let her run upstairs to her room.

"After the club, we're going to pay a visit to Heath Laurier." I examined Bosco, Macsen, and Banner all gathered in the hallway.

"Armani has business. He can't make it tonight," Bosco explained.

My men scattered throughout the premises were on high alert. Albe my butler and second in comman strode through the front entryway. "Celebrating in a public place is not his favorite thing, our baby brother is a loner."

"Is she coming?" Bosco asked and gulped down the remnants of the scotch.

"Lucinda has scared her. I have to allow her some breathing room. Today was a wake up call with her running to Heath."

"I heard you went to your playroom," Bosco joked.

I pointed a finger in his face. "Worry about your dick not falling off." Silence filled the room. Albe handed me a form to sign. I looked at what had their attention and saw Penelope come back wearing a short red mini dress showing off her legs. I remembered the sounds of her whimpers with my hand on her ass. I smirked and extended a hand to help her from the last step, escorting her from the house.

Everyone got in the vehicle, and Macsen pulled out of the driveway with security in front of and behind, as extra protection followed. Bosco answered his phone, placing his glass on the side of the limo cupboard. I rested a hand on her thigh, running up and down, while she stared off.

Cars were parked along the streets of the nightclub near the city. The nightclub was one of our biggest ventures, with investors wanting in after we expanded so fast. The music bounced, keeping people enthralled and ready to spend their money. Penelope relaxed under my grasp while I took the lead from the back employee entrance. Banner came from the back, Macsen in the front. Bosco reserved the top VIP area and invited a few people he knew. I kept Penelope at my hip and helped her walk upstairs and sit near the bar area in the corner. Our own private bottle girl and bartender already had drinks set up. Colors of gold and black etched around the room.

Bosco slapped one of the girls on the ass and pulled her

into him, whispering in her ear. Penelope sat protectively close to me with her legs crossed.

I spoke in her ear. "Enjoying yourself?"

"Just taking in the club. It's yours, correct?" Penelope asked, then put a glass of champagne to her lips.

I smoothed a hand up the back of her neck, inhaling her sweet perfume. "One of many."

"Do the employees know you're a killer?" Penelope pretended to ignore my touch, while I brushed my lips against the back of her ear.

I threw my head back in laughter. "Killer."

Her brows furrowed. "I have to get used to your life-style, right, Mr. Calabresi?"

I bent in close to her ear and extended my palm around waist with gentle pat on her hip. "You like pushing my buttons."

She mumbled under her breath and shifted in her seat. "Shit."

"Giosuè." All eyes glanced at the corner of the entry at security calling my name. My mind traveled to how he was even able to get close to our place of business. Any member of the Bulgarian cartel should have been turned down.

I stood. Penelope grasped my hand, stopping me. "Sit here."

"Wait." Penelope dragged her eyes from me to the man that stared at us.

"It won't take long."

"No, I—" She was momentarily speechless.

"Penelope, you're safe." I inspected her closely in reassurance, raising her palm to press a kiss against it.

"There's something I need to tell you."

"Give me a moment." I removed her hand, and Bosco

strolled up with his hand in the air, blocking Penka, the cartel's right-hand man.

I walked forward, stopping in front. "Penka."

Penka clenched his teeth, glanced at Bosco's hand, and back at me. "We need to talk."

"Not tonight and summoning me will never work."

"The garage business is looking funny lately. How much money is it costing you, now that Matevi is gone?" The hardened mask he held switched into a smile.

"More than one way to make money, Penka. You know a Calabresi never stays down long."

Although he was outnumbered in here with my people, it might still be a challenge that would end with bloodshed down the line.

He looked off and I followed his line of sight. "Pretty one." The teasing in his voice caused a tinge of possessiveness to rise in me, like it had earlier, with Heath.

"Keep your eyes off her."

He grunted. "Penelope Hutton."

I swiped my gun from my holster, a few of my men charged in closer.

Bosco pushed Penka back, blocking me. "Calm down, Giosuè." Bosco knew my temper would make the entire place shut down.

Penka held a taunting smile. "Paraskeva Abadjiev knows her very well."

My back stiffened at his statement. Bosco shook his head, knowing that I would be ready to kill for her.

I placed my gun back on my hip and pointed in his face. "Leave or get thrown out."

"Agree to meet again to negotiate a split," Penka expressed.

"Bosco will call you," I barked and pulled Penelope

from the couch, gripped her face and smashed our lips together.

Penelope cradled her arms around my neck. "Mmmmh-hh…" A powerful force passed between us, a wild sexual heat.

I pulled back and pecked her on the lips again. "How do you know Penka?"

Penelope reached her finger to my face to remove her lipstick. "Business."

I tightened my grip on her hips. "Penelope."

Penelope squirmed to get out of my hold. "If you can't handle my past, Giosuè, then don't ask me."

"Your past has weight on how your future goes, being a friend with my enemy is a problem."

Penelope relented and crossed her arms in a pout. "We went out one time for a dinner and I left two hours later because he tried to force himself on me."

I wasn't sure what she meant to me. Anytime I heard about someone trying to hurt her, I got protective. I released my hold and inched her toward the edge of the balcony, looking down on the club.

I kissed her on the left shoulder and felt her body relax in my chest. "I will handle him."

Penelope whirled around. "Are you planning on hurting every man I had a date with as an escort?"

"Is that wrong?"

"Yes!" Her cold resentment vanished.

Penka, Lucinda, and anyone else thinking taking control of my business will be easy never learned. Penka got the hint and left after a brief back and forth with security. Bosco's woman started dancing with him. I watched Penelope move her hips and sway her head left to right with the music. Taking a shot, I looked at Bosco and motioned at the time figuring now to move on threats since they seem to be in communicating together in some capacity.

The bottle girl handed off my alcohol, and I sat and watched Penelope move her hands and feet to the beat of the music.

"We're going to dance. Do you want to come?" Bosco's girl probed.

Penelope looked at me and I shook my head.

"She's fine right here."

"Giosuè, you're no fun." Saikina scoffed and strolled back to Bosco, causing a mini fight between them.

"Are they a couple? I never heard of Bosco being with anyone," Penelope wondered.

"He's single."

"She very friendly." Penelope and I chuckled, watching Saikina kissing another girl in front of Bosco.

"That's what he likes."

"So, you're not into sharing?" Penelope asked.

I slid a hand up her skirt, inches from her pussy, feeling the warmth of her voice go quiet.

"What do you think?"

Penelope's head fell back onto my chest, and she raised her hand to stop me from moving forward. "I think you will have people wondering what's going on over here."

I grazed my finger across the thin lining of her panties. "Let them wonder, Little Dove."

Penelope turned to face me with interest. "Giosuè, you're dangerous and out of control."

I grinned and eyed her cherry red lips. "You have no idea."

Chapter 10

Penelope

Seeing Giosuè sitting at the late-night café felt weird because he seemed like a snob who only had expensive taste. Going to a rundown burger joint after the club seemed out of place for him.

I sipped my water. "I had a good time tonight."

"I'm glad."

"Are you going to really hurt my friends?"

"Should I?" Giosuè watched me.

I picked up the loose pickle and tossed in my mouth. "No, they've been nothing but supportive of me since I met them after my grandmother died."

"How did you and Lucinda meet?"

I shrugged. "She was just there. Once my grandmother died, I tried to keep up with the bills on her house but living alone at sixteen would have been a lot for anyone back then."

"No other family members?" Giosuè passed a napkin to me to wipe my mouth.

"None. I tried to learn from my grandmother if I had cousins, but everyone just disappeared. After losing the house, I got a motel room from an older guy who thought he would get lucky, but I paid him dust. I worked in fast food while going to school, but of course, they found out about my situation and put me in foster care."

"Anyone touch you?"

I bit into the cheeseburger and moaned. "Not at first, but I'd already ran away and Lucinda happened to be at the motel talking to some other girls."

"She approached you first."

I nodded. "At first, I felt like she saved my life. She'd given me money to pay for the room for six months and seemed nice."

"She was testing you."

I sank back in the booth, dropped the sandwich, and drank more water. "I know that now and wish back then I could have seen the signs."

"At what point did you live under her at the mansion?"

"A few months after I graduated high school. I was around eighteen, going on nineteen, and I got into college. Only thing I did was go on dates. She always paired me up with men that held a lot of power."

Giosuè's jaw clenched. "The hotel."

"I had the dates at the hotel. Over time, Lucinda got jealous of the attention and men wanted to contact me directly, so I moved out on my own and got a condo."

"Lucinda worked a deal to try to sell you off to Heath."

"I gathered that when Heath was trying to get me to be with him more and with my other clients less."

"Mr. Calabresi, would you like anything else?" An older waitress filled his coffee cup, and Giosuè waved his hand in the air.

"Well, interesting to see you here." Alden and his team-mates stared me down.

I started to stand. Giosuè glared at me. "Alden, sorry. I should have checked in when you got hurt."

"You don't owe him anything."

"She's the reason I got shot," Alden grumbled.

Giosuè pulled out a gun and put it on the table, then stood. "Fuckboy, get out of her face before you end up in a body bag."

Alden's friends stepped away.

I gasped. "Giosuè!"

"I thought I knew you, Penelope." Alden's face contorted in a frown.

I jumped up and got between him and Giosuè, praying that it wouldn't bring more attention to us. The frustration in his eyes told me that I was wrong for getting in the middle because he grabbed my wrist and nudged me behind him.

I relaxed as the police entered the café. They stepped over in our direction.

"Is there a problem here, Calabresi." The police kept their hands near their guns. Maybe this would be the moment when I could leave and not have Giosuè follow me.

"No problem on my end. We were just leaving." Giosuè stretched his hand out to take mine, leading us out of the restaurant.

Looking back at Alden's scowl showed he would have made a bigger scene if given the chance. Aspen and Lucy always told me Alden never had my best interest at heart. So many times he tried to play me around his friends like we were casually dating.

I kicked off my heels as soon as I got back to my bedroom. Giosuè headed straight to his office without saying another word to me. My past played a part in my trusting him, even if he thought protecting me got him closer to hurting Lucinda. I ambled to the bathroom and picked up my makeup remover for my face. I clipped a pin on my hair, tossed the rag in the trash, and turned to set the temperature on the shower when a knock at my bedroom interrupted me. I strolled over and pulled it open. Maggie stood with a phone in her hand.

"Miss Hutton, I was told to give you this before I went to bed."

I stuck my head out of the room to scan the hallway. "Giosuè knows you're here?"

Maggie's laughter floated in the air. "He explained to leave it with you and to let you know rules are lighter for you as far as a phone goes."

I jumped for joy and kissed her on the cheek. "Seriously?"

Maggie rubbed my arm in comfort. "Yes, if you would like to spend time with your friends tomorrow, he will be busy with work, but extra security will be with you."

"Thank you."

"He's relaxed with you around more," Maggie informed me.

I waved goodnight. "Have a good night, Maggie."

"You, too, Miss Hutton."

* * *

My thoughts seemed to scatter. Aspen snapped her fingers in my face and I realized I had drifted off again. Shopping was a form of stress relief for me; it made me happy. For the past thirty minutes, Lucy tried on three different dresses and shoes to wear for a party that she wanted us to attend. Since the night at the club, Giosuè had increasingly stayed away from me. I felt a little offended, which was weird because he'd forced me to be at his place, while they tried to track down Lucinda.

"The skirt with those stockings looks good." Aspen ran a hand over the skirt in Lucy's hand.

Lucy shuffled from left to right, rocking her hips in excitement. "Brings out my eyes."

When the girls heard my voice on the phone it felt like old times of us just venting and catching up on our lives.

"So, you know, after my hospital stay, my parents kept me under lock and key," Aspen remarked with a hiked brow.

I embraced her in a hug. "Sorry, Aspen."

She tucked a blouse back on the rack. "Don't worry, I wanted to help you."

Lucy slipped a foot in a pair of blue heels. "It was kind of fun and exciting." Lucy put the shoes back.

I glanced away and shuffled over to the row of dresses hanging on the wall. We were at Chanel, near the food court. Lucy stood next to me, took another pair of leggings, and held them up under my neck.

"Try them on."

"Today is about us finally spending time together. I know you can't really talk about your situation," Aspen said, catching Lucy's glare.

I sighed. "My internship signup is coming up, and I'm trying to finish school."

Lucy roped an arm around my shoulder. "So, you can graduate on time, right?"

"Long as I turn in my papers on time, I will be able to walk. Being back in class feels good." I took the leggings from her hands and walked to the dressing room to try them on. I put my bag on the seat and changed. "The party's on campus."

"Last party of the year. We have to go out big." Lucy stood on the other side of the dressing room.

I pulled my shirt up to get a full view of the leggings. "These look great on me." I turned in front of the mirror.

"How do they look?" Aspen yelled.

I removed the clothes and put my regular pants back on. "Cute. I will take them."

"Hopefully I can get laid before I start my summer job," Lucy muttered, making us both laugh.

I walked out and shut the door. "Can we go eat? My stomach is touching my back." I rubbed my growling stomach.

Lucy giggled and bumped me on the shoulder.

After I paid for my clothes, Aspen took her bag of items from the cashier and strolled away, meeting Macsen and Banner at the front of the store.

Lucy locked her arm in mine. "Rather order once we get to my place."

I handed my bags to Banner. "Macsen, we're hanging out at Lucy's place and I can get ready from there."

"No more locking you away!" Aspen joked.

"With the amount of security following me now, Lucinda would be stupid to try it again."

Lucy living near campus made it easy to coordinate our evening. Giosuè texted a few times to check in on me, and I replied, keeping it short.

> **Me:** *Hanging with Lucy.*
> **Giosuè:** *My meeting is running long.*
> **Me:** *I had fun at the mall.*
> **Giosuè:** *What did you buy?*
> **Me:** *Clothes.*
> **Giosuè:** *Do you want to be punished again?*

Me: *Do I get to choose?*
Giosuè: *Keep playing around.*

"You're so wrapped up in the phone. Keep your head up for me," Lucy grumbled, curling my hair.

"Sorry, Giosuè keeps texting."

Me: *I have to go.*
Giosuè: *Be a good girl.*
Me: *I will try to behave.*

Aspen shimmied out of the bathroom, wearing the outfit from the mall. "I texted an Uber for tonight."

I threw my hands up in frustration. "Macsen is not letting me in an Uber, Aspen."

Aspen stomped her foot. "We show up in a limo and everyone will start asking questions."

"I think it's too risky."

Aspen sat in the chair, propped her head on her elbow, and watched us get ready.

"Finished." Lucy put the brush down.

I whirled in my seat to look at my hair in the mirror. "Love it, Lucy."

"You are so welcome. Let me get dressed, and we're leaving," Lucy said.

Aspen handed me a drink and we cheered to a great night. I stared out the window at the streetlights and the passing cars, and I thought about how my life had changed since the day I first met Lucinda, all those years ago.

* * *

I stepped off the bus and strolled home after an exhausting night of working at the Burger Den.

"You don't look like you belong here, sweetie." Lucinda blew smoke from her cigarette.

I slid the key in the door of the motel. "Uh, who are you?"

She cackled and stuck her hand out. "I'm Lucinda."

* * *

"Hey where'd you go?" Aspen checked.

I gulped my drink. "Huh?"

"Zoning out again."

"I never told you about me living alone after my grand-mother died."

"No, but we understood you weren't ready to tell us everything."

I expanded my arm around her back, pulling her in for a hug. "Having you and Lucy as friends mean the world to me. I am grateful to you both."

"No more sadness, we are graduating soon and you need to relax."

Lucy came out of the bathroom in full makeup, with her hair done, clasping her clutch. "Ladies, let's go find a man."

"Well, one of us already has a man, another has a stalker, and you... Well, that's a different story," Aspen joked.

"Bitch!" Lucy and I spoke at the same time.

We all fell out in laughter.

The line to get in the party was wrapped around the building near the sandwich shop close to our hang out. Macsen let us out from the truck since I was shut down on getting a Uber and Banner went to park. Aspen, Lucy and I chatted about how we planned on spending the summer if either of us ended up not working. The doorman gave us a wristband and passed a tray of shots at the door. Lucy took three and passed each of us one.

"Here's to the night of memories." Lucy beamed, drinking the strong liquid.

I scrunched my face, downing the dark scotch. "That was strong, too much for me." I patted my chest.

"Come on, let's dance, and then get more drinks."

Aspen snapped her fingers. I bounced my head to the sounds of Anita. Some boys tried to dance up on us, and Aspen's boyfriend slid behind her, hugging her from behind. A large grin came across her face and I loved how much he treated my friend like a queen and couldn't wait for when they got married.

"Here. It is much sweeter." Lucy grabbed the red cups from one of the party sponsors.

"Are you planning on getting drunk?"

"We have all the time in the world on the count of three."

"One, two, three." I finished off the sweet vodka mixture and put the empty cup back down to take another one. College parties weren't my vibe for the longest time; I pretty much had to be dragged to most of them when Aspen or Lucy wanted to be carefree. Movies, dinner, and shopping were our go-to entertainment for the first two years.

A round of guys started a beer pong line in the kitchen. My eyes danced around the room, and I smiled at finally feeling as free as a normal girl with no problems—well, except the angry cartel boss who had fallen into my life.

Aspen's arms rose high and waved for me to join her near the couch with the rest of the girls from class. I took a spot and watched them pass a bag of ecstasy pills and joints between each other.

"Want to try one?" One girl held up the bag for my attention.

I pushed her hand away. "No thanks."

Aspen's boyfriend came up beside her and whispered in her ear, helping her stand up and leading her away.

"Where are you going?"

"I won't be long." Aspen winked at me, climbing the stairs.

Lucy popped a pill from the bag and gulped it down with water. "She's going to be all night." Lucy shimmied in her seat.

I fanned myself and stood to amble outside for fresh air. I stood on the side of the wall, scanning all the people coming in and out.

"You stare too long, and I might think you're a cop."

"Should a cop arrest you?" He exhibited the bad boy aura.

The tall, blond, blue-eyed guy with a buzz cut leaned his back on the railing next to me. "I'm Michael."

He held a hand up for me to take. Shame bruised my cheeks at even thinking about another man when I hadn't figured out the Giosuè situation yet.

"Yo, Mike! Come on, they're doing a wet t-shirt contest," one of his friends yelled.

Our attention swung toward his friend. "Go on without me."

I propelled myself to stand up straight. "Please don't let me hold you up."

Michael angled his back to the railing to close the distance. "What's your name?"

"Penelope." Tiny hairs on the back of my neck flickered.

"I take it you're a senior?"

I craned my neck, checking through the window to see

if Lucy was still partying. "What makes you think I'm a senior?"

Michael jabbed a finger to a banner hanging on the wall. "Because this party is only for seniors."

Both of us laughed simultaneously.

"Come on, Mike, they're doing shots off their stomachs." His friend clapped him on the shoulder.

Mike pushed off the rail. "I should go and make sure he doesn't get into too much trouble."

"You should." The idea of something with him sent curiosity to my head.

His friend drifted near us. "Hey, aren't you the girl—"

"No, you have the wrong person."

Mike shoved his friend to move along.

I sighed and started to walk off the porch to take a stroll when a familiar person stood near a car talking with a group of men.

"Devin," I mumbled, looked away swiftly.

Lucy grabbed my wrist, startling me. "Penelope, come on. The guys are picking a partner for free beers."

"Lucy." It made me even more puzzled and nervous that Devin had followed me to a frat party. It implied that Giosuè was right.

"Yeah." She looked back at me with a bright face.

I angled my head, and Devin was gone. "Nothing."

For hours we danced, drank, and watched a few girls make out with some of the frat boys from another school. At one point, Mike held a good conversation, but when I wouldn't put out, he left with his friends. Lucy and Aspen left with her boyfriend. Macsen took note of Devin possibly showing up. I kicked off my heels, removed my earrings and bracelet, and sat on the edge of my bed in thought, twisting my necklace.

"How was your night?"

I jumped up, nervousness soaring through my body. "It was fine." I clamored into the closet and yanked my robe and nightgown from the hanger.

Giosuè angled his body against the wall with his hands spread. "Heard you danced with a few guys." Giosuè walked farther into my bedroom.

I shut the closet and folded the clothes in my hand. "Is that a problem?"

He stopped right in front of me and gently roamed the back of his hand along my cheek. "Go shower."

"What are you going to do?" I felt my knees fading at his touch.

Giosuè stretched his finger against my chest and tweaked my nipple. "You need to be cleaned."

"Are you going to punish me?" It felt as if my voice had been stripped bare.

He grinned. "Is that want you want?"

Reveling in having his attention, I opened my mouth to speak. "I—"

"Devin was spotted." He changed the subject.

I swallowed the words sprouting on my tongue. "Where?"

"Trying to head out of town, my men caught him at the toll booth." He tempered his anger.

"What about Lucinda?"

Giosuè put his hand under my chin and made eye contact with me. "Still running and plotting."

"Does this mean I can go home soon?" Fortunately, he didn't notice the tremor in my voice.

"Take a shower and get some rest. Talk some more tomorrow."

I jerked my head out of his hold. "You can't keep me here forever."

He pressed a kiss on the edge of my mouth. "Goodnight, Penelope."

Steamy hot water poured down my back. I curled up into a ball and recalled every memory and every choice I'd made to come into contact with Giosuè Calabresi. Never had a man seen into my soul before.

Once I cleaned up, I turned the water off, took a towel from the railing to dry off, and stepped on the heated floor. I dumped the towel in the bin and put on the long gown, then a robe. I brushed and flossed for bed, still feeling the effects from drinking tonight. I dragged my feet slowly downstairs, went into the kitchen, opened the fridge, and grabbed a water bottle and some ice cream. I pulled open each drawer searching for a spoon. I popped the top, scooped a generous amount of chocolate chip cookie dough ice cream, and moaned.

I stepped out of the entryway, staring at the pictures on the wall near Giosuè's office. Finally, I came around the corner, relaxing my shoulders as I saw that the hallway was clear of his men. I knew some stood outside for protection.

Surprised to see his office door open, I poked my head in and saw that it was empty. I trailed my eyes over pictures of him and his brothers when they were younger, plus another five boys, along with an older couple I assumed were his parents who held a baby in their arms.

"Baby Guilianna, Italy," I mumbled the words on the back. I placed it back on the shelf and scooped up more ice cream. I strolled around to sit at his desk, pressed buttons on his computer when a low dinging sound like a new email was received.

"Stop snooping, Penelope," I muttered, contemplating

whether I should try to get information on him. I slouched back in the chair, laid the carton of ice cream down, and pulled on the bottom drawer, but it wouldn't budge. I tried the middle slot, which held normal pencils and papers and a few messages about business. Again, I reached to type on the keyboard, but nothing happened. I snapped my fingers, lifted the office landline, and started to dial out for help.

"Find out anything?"

I dropped the phone and rushed to stand. "I was just calling to check on my friends."

Armani stalked farther inside. "Cameras all around you, Penelope. Give me a reason," Armani said, grasping my arm.

"Let me go." The air in my lungs retreated to the back of my throat as I struggled to breathe.

"Life is too short. My family is off limits to your games." He seemed like a man who neither forgot nor forgave, like he craved the security of tradition.

"I wasn't doing anything—and besides, Giosuè has cameras everywhere. I doubt he'd have a problem with me being in here."

He released my arm, and I marched out of there and back up to my bedroom. I locked the door swiftly and crawled into bed, staring at the ceiling.

"Can't escape." I groaned, turning the light off. I still felt the need to try to dive deeper—even though it would only create more trouble for myself.

Chapter 11

Giosuè

Every inch of her curves melted in the clothes she wore; somehow, she even made a long t-shirt look sexy. Armani informed me of her late-night search in my office, but I'd already had her on camera from the moment she left her bedroom. I knew leaving her to seek out some answers would make her interest pique higher. Each of us had cameras because of our life in the business and the people we hired sometimes worked for the enemy to get in our good graces. I never left anything on my computer that could be used on me, especially out in plain sight. When we got word of Devin trying to skip town Bosco hurried to take him back to our dark room to find answers on Lucinda. My day was packed with people pulling me in multiple directions. I still had a meeting about Matevi, and Elio asked me if Penelope could come in and do the interview for the internship. At first, having the role as boss was a dream, but all my time was compromised, and I couldn't see Penelope whenever I wanted, which was becoming harder and harder to manage. The plan was to take her to Sinful tonight, an exclusive BDSM for members my brothers and I joined a few years ago. A membership cost around a million a year, and only people with high discretion could get in. Since I was the don, I had gotten to the top of the food chain.

I paced in circles around him, watching the tension in his neck throb. "Devin, I thought we had an understanding."

Ego and jealousy never got anyone what they wanted out of life. People like him hated to be humbled, and the moment Lucinda put him in charge of being her right-hand man, Devin saw himself as untouchable.

"Lucinda will forget you even existed, so why not tell me where she's hiding."

"Fuck you," Devin grumbled, trying to claw his way out of the chair, but both his hands and legs were bound together by ropes.

"I tried to give you a chance to save yourself."

Armani held him by the top of his head, holding a needle to his neck.

I bobbed my head to Armani. "My brother's going to give you a little medicine to help you out."

"No, just kill me! Nooooo." Devin's eyes fluttered and his head fell backwards from the drugs in his system. He grinned, eyes rolling back in his head.

"How much did you give him?" I screwed up my face at him moving too fast.

Armani pulled up his sleeve and showed off the heroin marks. "By the fresh marks on his arms, he should be happy."

With his eyes rolling, Devin began to drool.

Each enemy had something they liked to hide, or moreso a weakness, and besides Lucinda, drugs were Devin's habit. The tech team had researched him and found out that he'd started using drugs when he was in high school. Lucinda had found him outside school getting high when she hired him.

"Tell me, Devin. Where is Lucinda?"

He laughed, clenched his fists. "Lucinda's going to kill you and Penelope."

I bent down to make eye contact. "Is that what you think? Lucinda's some dangerous mastermind? Penelope's with me safe and sound."

Devin chuckled, tears pooling in his eyes. "Not for long."

"Did you find anything in his car?" I cut my eyes to Armani.

"A few bags of clothes and money, but nothing that can tell us where she's held up."

I raised the hammer, stopped near Devin, and smacked his cheek back and forth.

"Hey, you want some more? You need to get high to feel alive, huh? Mommy issues fucked you up, Devin. Daddy didn't love you," I jested.

"Fuck you!"

I angled the hammer and forced it down on his left hand. "Stop bitching and tell me where she is!" I shouted.

"Aghhhh."

I thrusted the hammer on his right hand.

"Kill me, please." Tears trickled down his cheek. To waste his final moments thinking that Lucinda cared about him would only prolong his pain.

I swiped the sweat from my forehead with the back of my gloved hand. "Give him another shot."

Armani took the needle placed at his arm and stuck him with more. He tried to move away, but one of the guards held him down.

"She..." Devin stammered, started to convulse, and went into shock.

"Again."

Armani stuck him in the other arm with a different mixture that brough him out of the zombie like state.

His chest heaved up and down, his breathing slowed, and he went still.

Armani checked his pulse and shook his head. Devin was dead and I still had Lucinda to worry about along with the Bulgarian mafia. I ordered the cleanup crew to come in and take care of Devin's body. Armani and I went upstairs and waited for Bosco to finish his calls.

"All right, thanks."

I watched as Bosco slammed the phone on the receiver.

"Any good news?"

Bosco bit his bottom lip. "Not yet. Did Devin spill any information?"

"No." Armani took the chair next to me.

"Then we need to—" Bosco paused, sitting up in his chair.

The buzzing of my phone interrupted Bosco. "Detective Bridges."

"I thought you should know there are a few cars pulling up to the facility," Detective Bridges informed me.

DEA Agent Foster and Bridges received a hefty fee every month to keep us aware. "How many?"

"At least four," Detective Bridges answered.

I pushed my sleeve back to check the time. "Thanks, and any clues on Lucinda?"

"She's gone. Ghost. All my contacts came up empty," Detective Bridges replied.

I covered the end of the receiver and spoke to my brothers. "Lucinda's accounts are almost wiped out."

"She still has a few powerful men that support her," Detective Bridges reminded me.

"All right, let me handle Paraskeva first."

"You are aware that if some shit goes down, I need to be kept off the books?"

"Never worry, Bridges. Your money is always protected as long as you protect the Calabresi family." We hung up at the same time.

Bosco motioned to the door, standing from the chair and waving for us to go downstairs. "Remember we can't kill him yet."

"That's what you think." Armani chuckled and patted his left pocket.

Everybody clamored downstairs to the main room, and Devin's body was removed.

"Bosco, ride with me. Armani, you take the position at the top." My brothers trailed the guards outside. I piled in the SUV headed to the meat packing district as neutral territory for meet ups.

Another vibration from my cell phone pulled my attention, and I whipped it out. I skimmed the message to see a picture of Penelope on campus with her friends.

Drivers made it in record time even with all the city limits cutting us off at the lights. I stepped out of the truck, skimming the streets from left to right, and I noticed some of Abadjiev's guards outside a limo.

"He's inside." One of his men pointed at the sign of the abandoned building we used to throw off police.

"Make sure Armani has backup." I told my security as Armani's car took off around the corner.

Bosco strode along, held a hand up to be checked for weapons, and put his hands down. "Guns aren't permitted, Giosuè." Abadjiev's men held a hand up.

I pushed through his security. "Then leave yours in the car. We're not on your turf."

Bosco wagged his finger, motioned to his gun, and forced them to back off. When we got in the building, silence filled the secluded space. We stopped at a room that used to be a kitchen, now stripped of supplies. Paraskeva was there, with his right-hand man and a guard behind him.

Paraskeva blew smoke into the air from his cigar. "Business must not be going well if you're throwing tantrums, Giosuè."

"My business is fine and has nothing to do with you, Paraskeva. Tell me why we're here."

Paraskeva cocked his head to the side, puffed his cigar, dropped it on the ground, and stomped it out. "For a long time, our businesses have crossed paths, and we've worked to have mutual respect."

"And?"

Paraskeva snapped his finger and one of his soldiers stepped forward and handed him a white envelope. He removed a piece of paper. "Seems to me you've stepped over that line. Armani has taken out some of my men." He handed the photos to me.

I glanced over the three pictures, then dropped them on the ground, expressionless. "Then he had a good reason."

Paraskeva grunted. "Only reason we haven't retaliated is because we feel money could be more beneficial."

"For who?" The scent of rustic pipes infiltrated the room.

Paraskeva started to walk forward, but his guards stuck a hand to his chest to stop. "Need I remind you of the last time we crossed paths?" Paraskeva bringing up the past shooting back in Italy between our rival families.

"Try it now and see what happens."

His teeth bore down on the inside of his cheek. "Temper. Temper. Cat got you all riled up."

"If you think we'll give you a percentage, think again." Those memories of some of my friends dying hammered in my head.

"Tell me what you can gain by starting a war—one you will never win." Paraskeva hadn't noticed a few of my men had creeped in from the back.

"Matevi is the one who owes you, not us." Bosco's mouth took on an unpleasant twist ready to battle.

"Matevi was handled," Paraskeva replied, his eyes on my brother.

I backed up to depart. "Take up your concerns with someone that cares."

"She's a delightful woman." Paraskeva grinned, mouth compressed in a flat line.

Hearing him bring up Penelope caused my anxiety to creep up. "What did you say?"

Paraskeva hunched his shoulders, clapped his hands. "Penelope Hutton, a very gorgeous woman."

I opened and closed my fist. "You're going into rough waters, Paraskeva. If I were you, I'd stop while I could still walk out of here alive."

Paraskeva shifted his gaze to his soldier on the right, gesturing for him to pick up the pictures from the floor. "Am I to believe you can't share the wealth or do I need to take it... amongst other things."

"Bosco, let's go."

Back in the day, old cartels had a natural respect for consistency in not stepping on each other's toes once they'd established your territory, but Paraskeva had crossed that line multiple times.

"Devin might be dead, Lucinda is not." His arteries throbbed in his neck.

I turned to look over my shoulder. "Do you know where she is hiding"

He cut his eyes in my direction. "Maybe, but it comes at a price. I mean, we both have something worth protecting."

"Games. You're playing games."

"Fifty percent of your business."

"Get the fuck out of here," I spat and started to charge at him when Bosco yanked on my arm.

His nostrils flared. "Then we have nothing else to talk about."

Bosco dragged me backwards and whispered in my ear. "Before we walk, think about what damage will happen once we leave here. I say ten percent."

Bosco slapped me on the shoulder to relax and stood beside me.

"Ten."

Paraskeva pressed his lips together, spat out on the ground. "Forty, and I will leave Penelope Hutton alone."

"She's not a part of anything."

"Is that what you tell yourself to feel better? Thinking you can move around and make decisions and not expect to see consequences touch your personal life?" He slipped a hand in his side pocket, removed a small envelope, and passed it to his associate to hand off to me.

"Open it," Paraskeva suggested.

"You're making a big mistake." One was of me standing with Penelope at a restaurant.

"As you can see, I like to keep an eye on all my friends."

"Like Devin, I eliminate all threats."

"Forty," Paraskeva said.

"Twenty—and that's my last offer." I tore the pictures up and stalked out of the room.

"What are you going to do?" Bosco checked, focused on security when we got back in the truck.

I bashed my fist down on the window dashboard. "I want him dead."

"Shit, Giosuè, we already have an issue with Lucinda right now." Bosco dragged a hand down the back of his neck.

I turned and got in his face. "Then find her now! If Penelope ends up in the middle, Bosco…"

"He won't play fair." Bosco sighed.

"Neither will I." I wheeled back to my side of the door, dialed a number right as our car pulled off to a nice distance, and hung up, feeling the car shake by the explosion behind us.

"Shit!" Bosco ducked down, looking through the rear-view mirror.

"Armani." The Bulgarians keeps underestimating me and will uncover soon enough I'm not the one to play around with. Armani had his men place a bomb in a mailbox near their car earlier. It was set on a timer that he'd activate once we left. I let Paraskeva believe we were in dire constraints, but we'd always been steps ahead. Penelope being photographed ticked me off, and I felt at any moment he'd use a weakness of mine.

Detective Bridges calling meant he'd get a tip of what went down and would be there soon to run the investigation.

"No evidence comes back to me or any of my men."

"I can't talk long We got the call," Detective Bridges responded.

"He's going to make a move, so get your people ready for bodies."

"The Calabresi name being in the news is not a good look."

"Elio is here. You can get him to be the front talker."

He groaned. "Giosuè, we've talked about you going off and destroying buildings."

"At least it was a small one."

Bosco rolled his eyes at my comment.

"Give it a day or two." Detective Bridges broke all the rules when it came to getting his money and made sure anything that would point back to us would disappear.

"One day. I want you to find everything on Heath's background," I demanded, loosening my tie.

"The congressman?" he asked.

"A candidate not in office yet."

"Giosuè," Detective Bridges grumbled.

"Your time is up, Bridges. I have another meeting to handle." I cut the line and slid my cell back into my coat pocket.

I received a confirmation from Bosco, who held his phone up with a picture of the Bulgarian men who had died in the explosion. I relaxed and thought of my next moves with Lucinda and Heath, the final two components to take out who could do harm to my baby.

* * *

The rain hurled down. Huddled under the umbrellas with Penelope next to me, we rushed into Elio's law offices. Since the meeting with Paraskeva a few weeks ago, I'd made it a point for us to spend extra time together. She was surprised when I picked her up from school and went to lunch with her. Coming here was the last stop of the day before we got ready for the club.

"Do you need a lawyer?" Penelope trudged through the door.

"I have three."

My attention settled on her ass in the tight blue jeans. I shook off the lustful thoughts and placed a finger on her lower back to trail next to her. Bosco went back to work on a plan of action to handle any blowback with Armani. Detective Bridges already texted, keeping me updated that my brothers were fine and nothing came attached to their names from the explosion.

Elio, along with his assistant, came to greet us in the conference room. Penelope removed her coat and laid it on the chair.

"Please have a seat, Penelope." Elio directed her to a chair. I withdrew it for her to sit.

Penelope planted her hands on top, clasping them together. "Thank you, but why am I here?"

Elio dipped his head in my direction. "My cousin convinced me you'd changed your mind about the internship here."

Penelope glared at me and reared her head back. "He did?"

"You are graduating soon, correct?" Elio pressed.

"I am."

"Then perfect timing. We have a few spots open. The firm is well stationed in the industry and if it's on your resume, then it can help get you to the next level."

Elio broke into details

"Thank you for the opportunity, but shouldn't you give it to someone more deserving who has already applied?" Penelope took the new employee folder from his assistant.

Elio flicked the top off the pen and signed her contract next to us. "I know your story, and you deserve to have the position as much as anyone else."

"But—"

"The decision is already made," I cut into the conversation.

"Elio, thank you again." Penelope smiled, lifted the pen next to her, and signed her name on the dotted line.

"The law firm is my second baby. We have offices in Chicago, my home base, Italy, Seattle, and here."

Penelope handed the contract over to his assistant. "I did read up on your background as a lawyer and I'm pretty impressed."

Elio stretched his hand for a shake. "Thank you, Penelope."

"All right, cut the shit, Elio, before I call your wife." The length of time for a handshake was to piss me off and I grasped her wrist and pushed his hand back.

Penelope giggled but I didn't see shit funny.

"My cousin likes to be the only boss in the room." Elio gathered his phone, pen, and keys.

"I've learned." Penelope frowned in a teasing manner.

I laid my palm on her thigh and rubbed up and down.

"Agnes, my assistant, will give you a tour, get you situated, and start you with small tasks."

"Thank you, Elio." Penelope picked up her purse and followed Agnes out of the conference room.

"She's smart," Elio remarked, sitting back in his chair with his hands folded.

"Tell me something I don't already know."

"Savio called me yelling about you fucking exploding one of the Bulgarians cars or something."

"Why is he calling you and not me?"

Elio jabbed the side of his forehead, leaning forward. "Because he wanted someone calm to talk some sense into your head."

I hunched my shoulders. "I had a productive meeting."

Elio poked a finger to his chest. "Giosuè, you're talking to me."

"Savio is the last person to get on me about pushing someone's buttons."

Elio sprang up from his seat. "My brother's wiser now with his wife and kids, less reckless."

"For now, because the moment someone messed with his family, he'd go ballistic exactly like I did."

Elio trekked out of the room. "I mean all of us have, but you're making decisions without thinking it through long term."

"So, what happened?"

"Savio informed me that not only is Paraskeva trying to take over your legal businesses, but he's working with some outside forces for the fifty percent idea."

"Fifty percent for doing nothing? Bosco got the deal with Matevi going—and *if* we do business with Paraskeva, then I told him ten percent to keep the peace."

Elio popped into his office, trudging to the bathroom.

While I waited, I picked up my phone and scrolled through my emails. "He thought I would agree because of the past war in Italy."

"He's overstepping and baiting you into a confrontation." The bathroom door opened. Elio turned the light off in the bathroom.

I tucked my cell away in my pocket. "Armani is watching him now."

"What about Bosco?"

"Working on Lucinda."

That bastard Paraskeva felt like he could make the rules, but he was only a don because his brother was in prison, and they had no choice but to make him step into a role that he was never equipped to manage.

"How is that going?"

"Devin is dead."

Elio trekked to the elevator. "Any information come from taking him out."

"No, only showed devotion to Lucinda, which isn't new. Paraskeva had photos of Penelope. He was basically threatening to take her out."

"Does Penelope know you killed Devin?"

The elevator stopped on his floor. We let a few people come out before we stepped on.

I slouched against the wall. "No, the less she knows the better on me."

Elio gripped the door before it closed to let another group step onboard. "At least you're moving a little easier with her."

Both of us went silent as the elevator descended to another level. A group gathered to leave when the doors opened.

"Locking her away would force her to hate me forever."

Elio's eyes darted to the elevator numbers moving down.

"The next piece on the agenda is killing Lucinda and Heath, then stopping the Bulgarians from thinking they can run us."

Elio stopped walking and grasped the side of my arm. "No more killing."

I started to trail through the lobby. "Elio."

"I'm serious, Giosuè. The family cleaned up their name. To have the spotlight again will only mess up all our businesses, no matter the amount of money we have. Public opinion is important."

I clapped a hand on his shoulder. "I have you to worry about the image part."

My cousin loved to preach and get into my head about the best ways of dealing with problems besides bloodshed. I was used to telling Armani the same thing, but he always wanted to remind me of how I behaved a few years back.

Elio nodded at the lobby receptionist. "Never necessary to kill an enemy. Break him down in other ways."

"I know but blowing them up gets my point across to everybody at once." The sun shot out through the dusty clouds of rain.

"Take your girl and go home."

"We're heading to Sinful later tonight."

"Introducing her to your dark side?" Elio's security arrived in front of his building.

"When's the last time you hung out at Sinful?"

Elio tapped me on the chest, and we shook our goodbyes. "A year at least. Cora and I work too much."

"Find some time to play. Remove the stress from your mind."

Penelope appeared, laughing and hugging Agnes goodbye.

Elio peered at Penelope waving. "Is she ready for that life?"

"I'm taking things slow, but she's a part of my world and I can't let go."

* * *

Penelope sat quietly in the car after we left dinner. The meeting with Elio went great. I had a surprise for her and got her a new dress; it was a silky silver wraparound dress that had a split down the back and the side. Her hair was dolled up in long curls, and she was wearing light makeup that elevated her soft features. I explained tonight was just about looking mostly and I wouldn't touch her or allow anyone else to get too close. Elio made a great point earlier; I needed to let my walls down when I was around her and give her a different version of myself for once, without all the toxicity. Hopefully, she would see that every decision was not just a rush to hurt her in any way but to gain her trust.

The light mist from the rain still seeped in the atmosphere and onto the ground. I led her from the car and told my team to hang back, and I would buzz them when we were ready to go. After checking in at the door, Penelope took my hand, and we moved through the hallway of the club.

"Mr. Calabresi nice to see you again," Nicole the assistant Director of Sinful said.

"You too Nicole, how is everything tonight?"

"Everything is to your liking."

"I brought a guest tonight."

Nicole clicked on her iPad and pulled up Penelope's documentation.

Penelope popped her hip to the side and crossed her arms. "Consent form, background check. You ran a check on my medical files?"

"Is that not what you asked Mr. Calabresi?" Nicole prodded.

I nudged Penelope to the side. "I run background checks on everybody that works for me."

"I never asked to be here."

"But you don't want to leave."

"How do you know?" Penelope sassed.

I smirked. "Sign the form and find out."

Penelope hesitated for a moment, glanced over my shoulder at Nicole, and rolled her eyes.

"Are we ready?" Nicole pushed the iPad close to Penelope.

Penelope gripped the iPad, typed her name in, and passed it back to Nicole. I raised her palm and kissed the back of her hand, then trekked farther into the club.

Both of my brothers knew tonight my phone was not to be called unless there was an extreme emergency.

Chapter 12

Penelope

My jaw was on the floor. I couldn't take my eyes off her as she squrimed, crying out for more of his pain. The low music took some of the volume away, but mostly all the attention was on the couple in front of us. A large black panel lifted from the floor and a bed was set in the middle with gold and white trim. She was lying on her back with both her hands and legs tied up, and her eyes covered. She was wearing only red lipstick and high heels. I shifted from one foot to the other, remembering the chills from the spanking that left me in need.

I extended my pinkie finger around Giosuè's, peering at him. "She's not allowed to touch?"

"No. If she does, then she's punished. Giving her pleasure and pain is his job as a Dominant."

I watched him bend down close to her ear and whisper something, her mouth opened and then closed as she bit her bottom lip, and he pressed a kiss on the end of her ear.

"Here, take a sip." He handed me a glass of champagne and pulled me close to his side. The staff wore gold and white, an entire bar sat in the back corner, and high on a platform with stairs was a balcony that looked down on the main floor.

"How long have you been a member?"

"A while. Come on, let me show you around."

The crowd moved as Giosuè took me by the hand, leading me to a dark hallway. Each door was labeled with a number. "What do the numbers mean?"

"The numbers match what people have a taste for. Like, a five is for a threesome, or a twenty is for knife play."

With ease, we climbed on an elevator. He pulled out a gold credit card and scanned it to light up a button that led to a private room.

"Where are we going?"

"Have you ever been watched?"

"No."

"People pay to watch others and being a gold card member I have access to everything. We're going to the next level that showcases blood play."

"Is that one of your kinks?"

"One of many. I never take it too far unless my sub likes it to a heightened level."

The elevator stopped to let us off and more music played. There were only three rooms on this floor, and loud screams came from each one.

"When I let us inside, there is no turning back. If you can't handle what you see, let me know."

I ran a hand down his arm. "I can handle it."

Giosuè turned the handle and waved for me to peek inside. My mouth fell open in shock at a man holding a knife under a woman's breasts as blood trickled down. Another man was on his knees eating her pussy as she screamed and moaned.

"Deslin is another Dom with a sub at the club—a CEO of a Fortune 500 company," Giosuè explained.

Deslin glanced over, taking me by surprise when he licked the blood off the knife.

"She'll receive after care once they're done."

Deslin drew the knife down the woman's stomach.

"Yes, Master," she moaned.

Giosuè led us out of the room. "Have you ever been fucked by two men?"

"No."

Giosuè cradled my chin. "Good because I don't share."

I stared over at the paintings on the wall of women in different positions and scanned the large windows with black curtains hanging down. Giosuè removed his keys, wallet, and shoes. The black swing nailed to the wall and table next to the window piqued my interest. My hand moved across each item.

I whirled around and stopped him from walking farther. "What if I said I want you to please me like the woman I saw downstairs."

Giosuè stared at me for the longest time, and I felt like a fool for begging to be touched by him.

"Take off your clothes and get on the bed."

My senses reeled, as if I were short circuiting. The massage of fingers along my skin sent currents of desire through my body. He roused passion that I never had from my ex-boyfriend. It seemed like the sight of my bare skin and soft body had him unbearably entranced. Taking his cue, I slid the tip of my finger across his shoulder, making myself familiar. I couldn't take him teasing my nipples with his tongue. He smirked, released them, leaned forehead, and grasped my chin.

"Once we take it there you and that pretty pussy are owned by me."

His hands cupped my pussy.

"Giosuè, wait."

"Do I have your permission to own your body, Penelope Hutton?" Giosuè walked us to the bed.

I nodded.

He snatched his hand away. "No, say the words."

I begged, gripping the edges of his shirt. "Why are you doing this to me?"

"Say, 'yes, sir' when we're in the bedroom or my playroom. Do you understand, Little Dove?"

I could barely breathe. I felt his thickness near my opening. "Yes, s-sir," I stammered.

Giosuè slowly unbuttoned his shirt, removed his cufflinks, stepped off the bed, and unbuckled his pants while staring at me.

"For tonight, I will have you here. Next time we can go to the playroom."

"Will you hurt me?"

"I like to dominate, Penelope, but I would never do anything to hurt you. Sometimes I do knife play, blood play at the club."

I furrowed my brows, feeling jealous at him doing those things. "With other women?"

"That's the past, Dove."

"Better be," I muttered. He chuckled and moved back on the mattress, grabbed my leg, pushed it wider, and then his hand went to my ankle—kissing each side. Gliding his calloused palm across my abdomen I arched my back in silent invitation to be fucked. I hadn't been with a man his size before. One that seemed to ooze sex. Suddenly, he lifted my right leg and placed my body flush underneath him, while simulating thrusting in and out of me.

I wanted him in my mouth.

"Stop teasing me." Heat uncurled in my abdomen.

"I want your taste dripping down my throat. I want to fall asleep in your remnants and wake up in your essence every day."

"God, you're crazy," I groaned.

"Baby, crazy is sane in my world." Giosuè curved a finger around my hand and brought it to his dick. "Do you feel him? Ready to have these ten inches fill you all night and day, Little Dove?"

"Yes! Right now," I begged, smacked the bed, and tried to grasp the top of his boxers to pull them down.

Giosuè pushed my hand away. "Nope, I want your pussy in my mouth first." I could smell his wild, predatory scent as his head burrowed into the hollow of my collarbone. He peppered kisses along my neck.

"I give all of me." My chest rose and fell in ragged breaths. I watched him, my eyes in narrow slits as he inhaled the scent of my pussy. I wanted him to drown because of the wave of ecstasy throbbing through me. I tried to grip the back of his head but he held both hands down by my side. I squirmed at each lick and suck.

"Right there, ohhh-I-I," I cooed. I knew I should run from him.

"What do you need?"

"I need you."

"Right here this pretty pink nub poking out and calling my name." Giosuè pinched my nipples and separated my lower lips. All I had left to see was his head, moving up and down as I shattered into a million stars at the right amount of pressure and pain he placed upon me.

The feel of him brushing my legs caused my stomach to clench at what was going to happen next.

I lifted my head up to see his movements. "Will it fit?"

His head fell back at my comment.

Was I embarrassed? I've never had a guy this big.

Giosuè drew close enough to kiss me. "She's wet, warm, and ready for me."

* * *

Even though the night with Giosuè at the BDSM club continued to replay in my memory over the next few days, we spent more time talking and learning about each other's lives. I was an only child, and Giosuè was a big brother and leader in his family, which was admirable. Elio's assistant called me to get my schedule laid out a week ago and today was my first day going into the office as an intern. Mostly, I would be shadowing the assistant to one of their top lawyers to learn the ropes.

"Elio is out today, and I explained you will follow me today and be assigned to Mark Sanchez, one of the partners," Agnes explained.

"Mark Sanchez." I gathered my courage, held up my notepad and pen, ready to start.

Agnes poured cream in her coffee. "You were at the top of your class. What made you pick here for an internship?"

Agnes offered me a cup, and I declined.

I lifted the water bottle in my hand. "Elio and Giosue made it seem like the best place to be."

"Elio's a great boss."

"Um, he seems nice."

Agnes snapped her fingers. "Oh, yeah he did mention you being important and to not leave you alone."

I chuckled and scratched the top of my brow. "How long have you worked here?"

Agnes strolled out of the employee lounge. "Ever since I graduated, so about four years." She motioned to the cubicle area where I would be stationed.

"Nice. Any plans on becoming a lawyer?"

"Nope, I like the paralegal part."

I dropped my purse and notebook on the table.

"Come on and let me show you the offices and mail room." We glided around the offices and checked with each senior partner to let them know I was new at the firm. When it finally hit lunch time Agnes reminded me it was time to eat.

"Usually, I have lunch at the café down the street. A few assistants get together."

"Sure, I can go."

"Perfect, let me grab my purse and we can leave." Agnes shut off her computer, took her purse out of the bottom drawer, and I held onto my bag and lifted my buzzing cell.

I placed the phone to my ear. "Hello?"

"Bestie, are you sitting down?" Aspen excitedly yelled.

I whispered into the phone. "Aspen, I'm at work. Well, technically lunch break now."

"The internship, right?"

"Yes, what are you doing?" I strode to the corner of the room, away from people who could stare at me.

"Me and Lucy want to meet up for lunch and tell you the good news."

"What good news?"

"I got a job!" Aspen screamed into the phone.

I jumped excitedly. "Congrats!"

Agnes waved at me, and I followed, leaving our floor and getting on the elevator.

"Give me a second, Aspen. The phone might go out. We're on the elevator," I said.

"Sure, no problem."

Agnes strutted through the lobby, motioning for me to turn right out of the building.

"What café are we going to, Agnes? Do you mind if my friends come?"

Agnes pointed down the street. "The more the better. Malt House at end of the block."

"Meet us at Malt House."

"Be there soon," Aspen let me know.

The walk down Washington Street during the middle of the day felt like a midday concert happening, with loud noises and people pushing left and right to get to their destinations.

Agnes came up to the entrance, and a few girls noticed us. Waving, she ran to hug them and introduce me.

Agnes gestured to the tall brunette, and she rolled her eyes. "Everyone this is Penelope, a new intern at the office. Be nice." Agnes shoved Tinsley's arm.

Tinsley sassed. "Agnes, shut up. If the girl can't handle me, that's her problem."

I held up my hand. "The girl is right here."

"Ignore Tinsley," Agnes whispered in my ear, then strolled in and took us upstairs to a table with menus laid out. Everybody crowded around, and I peered up to see Tinsley frowning in my direction.

Something about her felt off, like she hated me for no reason. Agnes ordered a round of drinks and food. I looked over the balcony and saw Aspen and Lucy coming up to the bar. I motioned upstairs, and they pointed in my direction, waving to let the bartender know that they were with me.

Our waitress finished writing the order for the fourth

girl in the group, then I placed my order. Aspen and Lucy did the same. They hugged me and sat down opposite Agnes and me at the end of the table.

"So, what is the first day on the job like?" Aspen grabbed the glass of water, taking a sip.

"Boring, but I took a lot of notes. Agnes is my mentor-slash-Elio's assistant."

Tinsley's eyebrows pushed together in confusion at my comment.

"So jealous you have an internship already. My parents are pissing me off about getting a job soon." Lucy cupped her chin and laid her arm on the table.

I patted her hand on the table. "It will happen, be patient."

Agnes thanked the waitress when she handed off her drink, and then she stuck her hand out to Aspen, then Lucy. "I'm Agnes. You must be Aspen and Lucy, the best friends."

"Nice to meet you, Agnes. I'm Aspen."

"What are you two in school for?" Agnes asked.

Aspen detached the straw paper and dropped it in her glass. "I want to be a teacher and Lucy has no clue." Aspen bumped Lucy on the shoulder.

"Fuck you." Lucy cackled, then flipped her off.

"Agnes, are you sure Elio wants new people aware of his family business?" Tinsley asked, taking a piece of bread and butter and popping it into her mouth.

I caught a slight sneer on her face before she quickly looked away to continue talking to her friend next to her.

Agnes wiped food residue from her lips and cocked her head to the far right to stare at Tinsley. They were having some type of nonverbal communication, judging by the firm glare that they held. Since I was new, I wanted to avoid conflict at all times. If anything got back to Giosuè, then it meant that I would have to be stuck in lockdown again.

"Come with me to the restroom." I scooted back, jumped up, followed Lucy from the table, opened the stall door, and used the bathroom. I checked my makeup in the mirror when someone else came in behind us.

Tinsley grinned. "You're fresh and new around here.I should let you know to be careful."

"Careful?" I repeated.

Tinsley smirked, leaning against the wall. She glanced to look at my reflection in the mirror. "Careful in case you get hurt."

"Is there something I should be aware about?"

"Elio got you the job, correct?"

I dropped my head, laughed, and twisted to one side to face her head on. "This is about you sleeping with Elio?"

Tinsley pushed off the wall and stepped to me. Lucy came over and stood next to me with her arms at her side. "Do we have a problem?" Lucy checked.

Tinsley rocked on her feet, tapping her chin. "The Calabresi family means a lot to me."

"Whatever you have with them is only business, so I think your problem is on you."

Lucy tilted her head to the side. "Anything else, Tinsley?"

More than likely, if Lucy weren't there, I would be fighting Tinsley over nonsense—but never in my life would I fight over a man. Tinsley turned to look in the mirror, pushed a hand through her hair, and winked at me, then walked out of the bathroom.

"Tell me you know what that was about?"

I relaxed my shoulders through a sigh. "Well, I do *now*."

"Spill the beans." Lucy tossed the paper towels in the trash.

We left the bathroom and headed back to the table. "Something about her."

"The guy you're dating, has he been honest with you? You currently work at a firm with a lot of women he's probably met." Lucy caught my hand to stop me before we got to the table.

"She's the one with the problem, not me and besides, we all have pasts, Lucy." I wouldn't dare tell her how pissed I was at being in a position to have confrontation at my job. After lunch was finished, Agnes paid for everyone, and we walked back to the office. I continued learning the ropes and setting up my desk.

Surprised at the person picking me up I took my time admiring him on the phone for a few minutes and then slid in the car.

The wind blew in my hair. Giosuè gripped the steering wheel of the Mercedes Benz, with me in the passenger seat, as we passed other cars on the freeway. A few minutes of ignoring his conversation finally ended, and he turned to stare at me. A small part of me wanted to ask him if Tinsley and Elio had a thing or if he knew her intimately. We all had a past; I had my faults and secrets.

"How was your first day?"

"Fine."

Giosuè removed one hand from the wheel and cupped my chin to turn and face him. "Is there a problem?"

"No."

"All right."

"How was work today?"

He swiveled my head to face him. "Fine."

I rolled my eyes at his childishness and felt my phone buzz in my purse.

Unknown: *Think you're safe from me?*
Me: *Leave me alone Heath.*

"Who's texting you?"

"No one."

"I have a few leads on Lucinda, and then I have business out of town, so the next few days I want to spend with you."

"Where are you going?"

Unknown: *Giosuè can't save you.*
Me: *If you-*

The phone was snatched out of my hand.

"Who the fuck is this texting you, Penelope and don't lie?" Giosuè read off the messages. I'd tried to ignore it for the longest time, but at that point, I had no choice but to tell him about the threats.

"I believe Heath is stalking me."

Giosuè held tightly to my hand. "Heath? When did these start?"

"A few weeks ago—and I forgot about them, honestly, but I think seeing me with you triggered him."

"Maybe him or Lucinda." Nervousness creep up on me.

"Lucinda wouldn't send text threats." Giosuè drove up to the gate of his home and pushed in the code.

"My brother will trace the number, for now let me handle him."

I reached for the handle to get out. "How will you proceed?"

"The less you know the better."

"Giosuè, you can't kill him."

Giosuè pecked me on the lips. "Who said anything about killing him?"

I watched him climb out of the car, saunter to the other side, and help me out of the car.

"The answer to everything with you is to kill the problem."

Giosuè threw his head back in laughter.

I pushed him on his chest. "And you're laughing."

"Are you scared for your little boyfriend." Giosuè stumbled back.

"No—and let me handle Heath. I have enough on him that he'll leave me alone."

Giosuè moved some of my hair to my back. "My job is to take care of you; no more talk about Heath. Go get washed up. We're going out tonight."

Albe opened the front door upon our arrival.

"To where?"

Giosuè handed his keys and coat to the housekeeper. "A dinner with a few business associates."

"Like other mob people?" I trailed him upstairs.

Giosuè stopped in front of his bedroom. "Something in that vein."

"Am I safe to be around them? I mean what if they want to—"

Giosuè pressed a kiss atop my forehead. "Hey, you're never not safe with me, Little Dove."

"Okay. I trust you."

"You have thirty minutes, and then we need to leave." Giosuè smacked me on the butt.

I turned the knob and propped the door open. "What type of dinner? Formal or casual."

"Wear something that's easy for me to take off you later!" Giosuè yelled from his room.

"Dressing for your pleasure then."

"Always, Little Dove."

We left his place and headed out again. I tried to dress comfortably and not too flamboyant since it wasn't a major event.

Security was behind us and on the side of the street when the car parked. Earlier, he'd told me it was an afternoon party, with a few businessmen and their wives from the art world. I pulled down my dress after checking my makeup in the mirror. The house was out in the Hamptons, far outside of the city, and a few times I had clients bring me as their dates.

"Are you sure I'm not overdressed?"

"You look good." The grin on his face told me I might end up bent over if I kept bringing up my attire. Without needing to show our ID, we walked through the mansion and a few waiters offered us something to eat.

"No, thank you," I declined and stuck close to Giosuè as he talked to a few of his friends and explained that he had a surprise waiting for me. Their home was large on many acres of land, and cars parked in the grass. I picked up a glass of champagne from the server and sipped on a drink to calm my nerves.

"Thank you."

A few women stuck together in the corner and talked. I felt like they wanted to say something but were hesitant to ask me over.

"Are those more wives or girlfriends?"

Giosuè looked in the direction I pointed.

"All wives."

"They look older than me."

Most of them were blonde, wearing diamonds around their hands and necks and long elegant dresses.

"You look just as good or even better."

"My little white and black skirt dress."

Giosuè pulled on the hem of my skirt.

"Stop before someone sees us." I nudged his hand away.

"You're the only one who's important here."

"You'll tell me anything."

We both laughed and walked around the living room, chatting with more guests.

Chapter 13

Giosuè

Elio held his hand up after thanking everybody. I watched the men hold hands with their wives and cheer to bigger opportunities as the founding dons of each family approved the latest plan to secure negotiations for the Calabresi cartel. The party in the Hamptons was full of mobsters and businessmen. Penelope relaxed and talked with the other women, and I stood back and watched, admiring her beauty.

"Stare any longer she might break."

I sipped the rest of the shot and laid it down on the table. "What are you doing out here?"

Tinsley licked her bottom lip and reached to touch my hand, but I pushed her away and stomped to the hallway. She followed me.

"Am I not a part of the Calabresi family anymore?"

I grabbed her chin and squeezed it. "Armani know you're here?"

My little brother handled where our soldiers should be at all times, so her being here meant that someone would be taken out at any moment.

"He does." Tinsley jerked back.

I poked my head back into the living room. "Who are you taking out?"

Tinsley ran a hand up my chest. "Luna Diaz."

"Why?"

"He's been short two times in the past few months." Tinsley leaned forward to kiss me on the mouth and stepped back.

Penelope was here and having her in the midst of a hit especially if it went wrong would piss me off. I reached into my pocket and dialed Armani, interrupting whatever he had planned to take on right then.

Tinsley started to walk off. I grasped her by the arm to stop her and waited for Armani to answer.

Armani said, "Brother, you know I'm busy at the moment."

"I'm calling Luna's hit off."

Armani grimaced. "Luna Diaz has to be taken out."

"Agreed, but not here."

"The reason for doing it at this party is to send a message," Armani argued.

I kept my hand on Tinsley's arm. "Penelope is here."

Armani hated anything dealing with feelings that interfered with business, and on some level I was the same, but now that Penelope had started to adjust to our lifestyle I preferred to keep any issues at bay.

"Have Tinsley come back to the city." Armani scoffed and dropped the call.

"You can leave now." I shoved my phone in my pocket and went in the direction of Penelope and Diaz's wife.

"She's pretty." Tinsley gripped my elbow.

My gaze roamed from her eyes down to her hand on my arm. "She's not your concern."

"You need someone who can help you in the cartel world. I'm not sure what *she* can do for you."

"Good thing I never take advice from you."

"Giosuè, please, listen to me."

I wrapped a hand around her wrist, twisted slowly, and removed her hand from my arm. She cried in pain, as I clasped a hand around her mouth. "Shushhh, never touch me again, understand?"

Tinsley nodded and I removed my hand from her mouth, scanning the look of anger in her eyes. "She'll never be the one for you."

"Neither will you." I marched out of the hallway, snuck up behind Penelope, placed a hand on her lower back, and kissed her cheek.

"Are you having fun?"

Penelope laid her head on my shoulder. "Mrs. Diaz used to teach art class before she got married."

"I was telling Penelope that we should have lunch one day. I have a few pieces that I bought from your gallery, Giosuè," Juliette noted.

"One day we can set it up. For now I have another appointment, so Penelope and I have to go."

"Aww, we just got here, babe."

I scanned the room, watching Tinsley stare back at me in a snarl.

"We'll come back. Elio has parties all the time."

Penelope reached over to Juliette, holding both arms out for a hug. "Nice meeting you."

"You too, Penelope." Juliette waved goodbye, and Luna shook my hand. I gripped it tight with a stern gaze. The smile wiped from his face.

"Armani will be in touch."

The look of despair ran down his face, letting him know

he'd made a mistake not paying on time and putting me in an awkward situation when he came up missing. Juliette had us over many times for dinner. She was an American woman, like Penelope, and she hadn't grown up in the cartel life.

The bodyguards lined up by their cars and signaled that it was time to go. Penelope got in the car, and I jumped in, not waiting for them to catch up, as I sped down the road.

If Tinsley made a move in sight of the other Dons, then I'd be brought in to answer for those choices because they knew she worked for us.

Penelope raked a hand through my hair. "Hey you look lost."

I trailed a kiss down her arm. "Business."

"I like Juliette."

"Don't get too close."

"Why not?"

"You're the head boss's girlfriend."

"Oh, girlfriend," Penelope teased.

Going back to my youth I never expected to be interested in becoming someone's husband, responsibility. My father taught us to be a protector. The nature of the cartel business was family loyalty; they were people who had our back—no matter how much of the world was against us. Penelope's poise, strength, and courage to challenge and question me meant that I knew she was the one I always wanted to see when I came home at night. She laid her soft hand on my chest, and I pressed a kiss on her temple, watching her and trying to see myself as a married man.

"Is that too much?"

"I'm surprised you want me to be your girlfriend. Seemed like the type to keep me around just for sex."

"Have I not brought you around my family and friends?"

"Yes, but—"

"You're the first woman to come to my home. My life is not for everyone to be included in or comment on. I'm very private."

Penelope turned down the radio as we eased up to the condo that she used to live in. My men stayed near their cars—except for Macsen, who trailed us inside. I clasped my hand around her waist, keeping her close.

"What am I doing here? Are you letting me move back home?"

"I have a surprise."

Penelope clapped her hands together. "In my condo?"

Macsen passed the key to unlock the door. He slipped inside and turned on the lights near the wall, He scanned the empty room except for the man sitting in the chair tied up from hands to knees, and his mouth covered with a gag.

Penelope froze then glanced over her shoulder at me.

"He's a problem I need to solve."

She turned to face me. "But—"

"He's threatening you."

Penelope blocked me with her hands up. "Heath is not going to hurt me. This is wrong."

Macsen and Armani had up scooped Heath after a late-night campaign rally. They'd picked him up on the drive home. Armani had made sure that we could make it look like an accident, and once we were finished, the body would be placed at his home. The news coverage would show him dying from a drug overdose. We had already set stories in motion to be planted as soon as we were done.

Penelope getting upset at me for taking his life would cause a problem between us.

"Arghh... no," Heath mumbled.

Macsen shot him with another needle full of heroin.

"Heath is not a killer."

"I told you I would protect you from anyone that tries to hurt you."

Penelope threw her hands up. "Heath, tell him that you won't do anything to me."

Macsen removed the cloth from his mouth. "I swear it was not me," Heath begged.

I cocked my head to the side and stared at him. "How long were you Penelope's client?"

"Huh." Heath hung his head back.

Macsen smacked him on the back of the head to focus.

"How many times have you sent her text messages from an unknown number?"

"Giosuè." Penelope moved in closer to him.

Heath shook his head and grunted. "Never, I promise."

"See, he answered. Now let him go."

Macsen stepped back and I ended the distance between me and Heath, bending down to look him in the eyes. "She's mine."

His eyes grew bigger when I removed the knife from my pocket.

"Wait!" Penelope jumped in, facing me, and blocked Heath from my line of sight.

"Take her out of here."

"Giosuè!"

Heath screamed as I cut him across the neck, heart, and down his chest. I watched his body go limp, breath slowly fading away.

I stomped off to the bathroom, cleaned the knife, then went out and found Penelope pacing back and forth in tears.

"Call the cleanup crew."

Macsen waved the guards over to step back inside I nudged Penelope to look in my eyes. "Those tears will no longer shed for another man."

"We could have turned him in to the police, Giosuè. You're making me an accessory to murder."

I smirked. "Baby, the police won't come for me."

"How can you be so sure?"

"Calabresi own the police, mayor of the city, and governor of the state. Plus, we have a few contacts in Homeland Security."

"Is he really dead?"

"Yes, no more keeping secrets from me. If anyone tries to contact you with threats, I need to know."

A white van pulled up with *Medical Examiner* written on the side, and a team piled out. Armani cut his eyes at me. Anytime I personally took care of a threat, my brother would handle the cleanup.

Now that Heath was out of the picture, Penelope could feel less guarded. Lucinda was still in hiding, but we were close to discovering her whereabouts.

* * *

I was standing in my office listening to my cousin rag on me about killing a congressman days ago, when we all knew a similar issue came about with Renato and his brothers in Chicago. Penelope calmed down after a deeper conversation, during which I explained that her safety was more important. Today, she was planning her graduation party to distract her from what happened, and I welcomed her to use my credit card. Heath's face was plastered on the screen, Bosco had his feet up on my desk, and Armani sat on the couch scrolling through his phone.

"It was a job you could have pawned off to me to handle," Elio fussed through a frustrated breath.

"Elio, you know if I let this go to someone else, it would eat me alive if a mistake happened."

"Are you saying we're unable to deal with your requests?"

I ran a hand down the back of my neck. "Stop whining about a decision I made."

"You brought her into it, dumbass."

"Fuck you."

"Yo! No one can curse my brother out but me," Renato argued in the background.

"Renato, watch your words," Armani yelled.

"Armani, you learned from me on how to hold a gun, little buddy. I suggest you stay mute," Renato joked.

Armani frowned, lifted his phone, and dialed his number. A few seconds later,

Renato showed up on a facetime call as we continued to talk with Elio.

"When are you coming to Chicago?" Elio questioned. The entire room went silent.

Armani stood with his phone in hand, arguing back and forth with Renato.

"Soon. Penelope has a graduation party and I have business with the Bulgarians."

"How is that looking?"

"Once I kill Paraskeva Abadjiev, business can resume."

Bosco stared at me.

"They're saying an investigation should happen on Heath."

"Hold up." I put Elio on hold, dialed another number on my office line, and merged the calls once they picked up.

"Agent Foster Raynor."

"This was you?" Foster challenged.

"Agent Foster, will we need to discuss any issues about Heath that may turn up?" Elio cleared his throat.

"Elio Calabresi," DEA Agent Foster said.

"I have you merged with my attorney."

Bosco's brows rose in curiosity.

"No problems on my end," Agent Foster replied.

"The Commissioner will be expecting a call from you. Make sure nothing falls back on my family, Agent Foster," Elio remarked.

Foster inquired, "Should I see a bonus coming soon?"

"Already transferring to your offshore account." I pointed at Bosco, waiting to get confirmation of the funds being paid.

He threw a thumbs up.

"Check your account, Foster."

"I will wait on confirmation. His file will be ruled a drug overdose and pointed at the Bulgarian cartel," I explained.

Foster stated, "That's not possible, Giosuè."

"Why not?"

"I have a few low-level junkies that I can pawn it off on; they have rap sheets," Foster insisted.

"No, the only way it works is if the Bulgarian cartel is on alert."

"Is there something going on that I should be made aware of? I mean, two rival cartel families going back and forth in New York is not what I need right now," Foster pushed.

"He might be right, Giosuè," Elio agreed.

Bosco motioned for me to mute the call.

I rubbed the bottom of my chin. "What are you thinking?"

"Putting word out that the Bulgarians had something to do with Heath might bring eyes on us. Foster is right," Bosco said.

I looked at my brother. "Then who?"

"Lucinda." He smirked.

"Completely wipe her out and have everyone looking for her."

Bosco agreed, "Exactly."

I pressed the unmute button. "I have another name for you."

"Is it a cartel boss?" DEA Agent Foster challenged.

"Lucinda," I responded.

"The Madam?" Foster raised his voice.

I sat forward in the chair. Foster thought I had him as my only resource, but we've had several steps in place to replace him if he decided to not do what we say.

"She's been an issue for our family," Elio informed.

"Lucinda has a lot of enemies. If we make her the main suspect, it might bring on a lot of heat," Foster expressed.

"Not our problem," Elio said.

I clicked to remove it from speaker phone, closed my eyes, and reclined in the chair. "Get it done, Foster, or more than you will be losing their jobs and life."

Elio spoke to someone in the background. "Keep me updated on any other moves you make."

"How's she doing?" I asked.

"Penelope?" Elio answered.

"Yeah, at the office."

"From what I hear she's doing great, learned the ropes quickly."

"Thanks for backing me up," I finished and stood.

Bosco came out of the office with me. I heard loud laughter throughout my house. The staff was running around with wide grins on their faces. This was the biggest party that I'd ever thrown for anyone anywhere—let alone at my home. I paused at the entry of the kitchen in awe of Penelope talking with Maggie. She stood on the side of the island with a notebook and pen.

Bosco pushed me aside, went farther into the kitchen, and reached for an apple on the tray. Penelope glanced at him and frowned.

"Hey."

I folded my arms, came close to her, and pecked her on the lips. "How is the party planning going?"

"Maggie is a great help. I should be done in a few minutes. I have the caterer coming at noon, flowers and decorations around two."

"I'm more than happy to assist, Miss Hutton." Maggie shuffled away from the kitchen.

"Please, Maggie, call me Penelope."

"Penelope it is."

Bosco leaned next to the counter. "How many of your friends are coming to the party and do they look like you?" Bosco asked, and I saw the sparkle in his eye.

"Watch it, brother."

He tossed the apple in the trash. "I admire her big brother. She's beautiful, which means her friends have to be good looking."

Penelope sat on the stool, writing on her notepad. "My friend, Aspen, is taken, but Lucy is single."

Bosco rubbed his hands together.

"Call me if you need anything else. Me and Bosco have to leave for business."

"Where are you going?" Penelope glanced at me.

I pecked her twice on the lips, then the forehead. "Can't tell you."

Penelope leaned up against my chest, gazed into my eyes, and wrapped her hand around my waist. "Well, do you think we can do another date?"

I rubbed up and down her back. "I think it can be arranged."

"Can you tell me where you're going?"

"No."

Penelope released her arms from around me. "Is it dangerous?"

"Being born a Calabresi is dangerous."

"Be careful."

I massaged her shoulder then caught up with Bosco to get business started on the next issue from my list.

Chapter 14

Giosuè

To make it comfortable for his people to relax at another meeting, I arranged for a visit to a club, with a few drinks that I hoped would settle them into a calm state. Two of the waitresses stood on the edge of the couch, with their breasts spilling out of their tops. A few of Paraskeva's men passed around drinks and cigar smoke escaped their lips. On the main stage, two women kissed each other, rubbing their bare breasts together.

"Exclusive club? How can we become permanent members?" The underboss checked.

"Becoming a member is only for people that are recommended by top clients."

Paraskeva rubbed along her thigh to her stomach. "For us to be here means you've agreed to our terms."

"Your terms interfere with mine; I already told you what percentage you will have."

Paraskeva briefly took his eyes off the dancer. "Do you think having us show up here will make me change my mind?"

"I couldn't care less about changing your mind. We're

both businessmen. What I'm proposing is a fair piece of the pie, and no violence will come if you agree."

"What do you want?"

"I need some of your contacts."

"For what?"

"I need to find Lucinda."

Paraskeva chuckled, stacking his arm on the back of the couch. "Why should I help you with anything?"

"Lucinda is going to be named as a suspect in a murder, and I have to find her before they catch her."

Paraskeva gritted his teeth. "Using my resources once again will costs you, Mr. Calabresi."

My eyes scanned to the center of the stage. A woman was lying on her back, getting her pussy eaten.

"Twenty-five percent," I suggested.

"Plus, access to ports—and I want in on the gun shipments," Paraskeva countered, his eyes roaming over the women walking by.

I glared at him and nodded. If my plan worked, then all my problems would be taken care of very soon.

"Do we have a deal?"

"I want your people on it now."

Paraskeva motioned one of his soldiers to him and whispered in his ear.

"Do you have a picture of her?"

I reached into my pocket, grabbed my phone, and scrolled to a photo of Lucinda. "I sent it to your phone."

Paraskeva slapped his hands together. "Now that that's settled, let's drink and watch the show."

I sat back, took in the section, and nodded my chin at Armani when he approached the VIP area. I gently moved one of the dancers out of my face and walked up to him. "You lock it down?"

"Tracking device on his car and the underboss's," Armani remarked.

"Good, time to go and wait."

I reached out to pat him on the shoulder, then whipped around to face Paraskeva. "Enjoy your time here. All the drinks are on me. The owner won't give you any problems."

Paraskeva waved off my words and let another woman straddle his lap.

I eased through the crowd with Armani, Macsen, and two more guards. We left the club and went to my limo at the back of the building.

"The tracker is on. As soon as he leaves, we will have all his locations," Armani explained, typing on his cell.

Bosco sat across from us waiting for us to leave. "Penelope wants you back at the house by six."

I glared at him. "Why is Penelope passing messages through you?"

He shrugged with a hint of mischief on his face. "She couldn't get a hold of you and Maggie called my phone."

I'd rather avoid fighting with my brother, so I sent a text to Penelope to check in on planning for the party.

Me: *I hear you're talking to my brother.*
Little Dove: *Well, you weren't answering my calls.*
Me: *I had my phone off in the club.*
Little Dove: *Wait, you went to the club without me?*
Me: *Business meeting.*
Little Dove: *Did you play with anyone?*

Macsen circled around the docks. I took in the shipment getting unloaded and waited until he parked in a secure spot.

Me: *It was business only baby.*
Little Dove: *Long as you kept it to business.*

I chuckled at her cute jealously creeping up. We came up to the boat as a few signed off on the count of crates. The light wind blew in the air as goosebumps formed on my skin at my plan to have Lucinda found was coming to end.

* * *

A large sign and balloons hung on trees and poles on the back of some chairs. Penelope's friends and a few family members she discovered through searching her father's side with my vetted lawyer came out. The first gift bag Aspen put next to the others on the table. Lucy stood beside her; they were laughing and joking together at Aspen's annoyance at her boyfriend, who was drinking and flirting with one of the waitstaff. The entire backyard color scheme of red and white complemented the red flowy dress with an off shoulder cut she tried to hide a few nights ago. The fact that she was my girlfriend, but she was trying to avoid showing me her outfit because she knew I would disapprove of it made me laugh. Mounds of trees surrounded the small gathering. Guards stood on watch in the front and back. I listened in on all the lively conversations, hearing my brothers Bosco and Armani in a heated argument. I didn't want it to get back to Penelope, so I stomped in their direction.

"The problem with you two needs to be done asap."

"Only problem we have is word got back to Underboss and Abadjiev thinks we're playing games and it might be a setup."

"How is that possible?"

I peeked over my shoulder to make sure no one was listening or Penelope caught word. Any business that interrupted her party would cause even more stress.

"Money makes people do stupid shit and Lucinda offered them Penelope to hurt you."

I glared at his statement.

Bosco tucked a cigarette in his mouth and took the lighter from his pocket. "Lucinda is working to hurt you and she knows the way to do it is by grabbing Penelope."

"Do you have her location?"

"Not yet. Abadjiev has it for sure," Armani responded, lifted his phone, and scrolled through his messages.

Penelope snuggled against my arm. "Today is supposed to be about me graduating. Are you three doing business?"

I extended my arm around her neck and pecked her on her temple. "Discussing the surprise I have for you."

"A surprise for me?" Penelope laid a hand on her chest.

I cupped her hand, brought it to my lips, and peppered kisses as she smiled and bit her lower lip. "We're going on a trip."

"A trip, just the two of us?"

"Once we have Lucinda, and I take care of some other things, I'm taking you out of the country."

Penelope's friend, Lucy, slid next to her, holding her hand out to Armani. "Hi, I'm Lucy."

"Not interested." Armani grunted and stomped away.

Bosco and I cracked up at the confusion on her face. "Ignore our brother. He hasn't eaten today."

Penelope shoved Bosco in the arm, turned to face me, and encircled her arms around my neck. I cupped the back of her neck. "I can tell something is wrong."

I bit my top lip. "You worry about what you're wearing on the trip."

She sighed, then slid a hand down my chest. "Promise to end whatever business soon, I worry about you."

"Lucinda tried to double cross me."

"How is she constantly getting people on her side?"

"Because she's smart and has a lot of information about people in higher places."

She groaned, dipped her head back, and blinked her eyes repeatedly. "Okay, then let me help you."

"No."

"She wants me, so use me as bait."

"Never a good idea to offer yourself up, Lil' Dove."

Penelope snuggled up under my arm. "Let me help you."

"Help me by having fun at your party." I gripped a hand on her waist.

"Thank you for throwing a party at your home."

"No one else could get a party out of me, not even my brother."

"That really means I'm special," Penelope tittered and bit her thumb sexily.

"More than special."

Aspen waved her hand in the air. "Penelope! Come and dance."

More food was brought to the buffet tables. Maggie talked with Penelope, and I watched the excitement of her cake being presented.

I touched my pockets and felt for my buzzing phone to answer.

"We got your package," Paraskeva says.

Penelope laughed with her friends near the pool.

"How do I know you really have her?"

"Sent you a picture," Paraskeva chuckled.

I held my phone away from my ear, scrolled through the

thread, and saw Lucinda outside a house in Philadelphia. "She's in Philadelphia."

"I can have my people sit on her for twenty-four hours. If you refuse to make the deal, then we ride away."

"Has she spotted you?"

"No."

"Send me the address," I demanded.

Paraskeva explained, "Not until I have the guns and drugs."

"Playing a dangerous game will end terribly for you."

"I'm prepared to walk away, are you?" He hung up.

I bit my bottom lip and put on a smile when Penelope stared back at me from the cake table. The DJ continued to play different tunes, and when a champagne tray came up from a waitress, I grabbed one and chugged it down. I came up behind Penelope, pulled her back to my chest, and pressed a kiss on her shoulder.

She lifted a fork and put a piece of cake to my mouth, then wiped the excess frosting from my lip with her finger. "I have to step out for a moment."

Penelope wiped her hand on a napkin. "Where are you going?"

I pecked her on the cheek, nuzzled my face in her neck. "Nothing to worry about."

"Why does it seem like you're not coming back?"

"I'll always come back; you never have to worry about me coming back."

Her sweet sent kept me coming back for more.

Penelope tugged on my hand. "If you are going to find Lucinda, I want to come with you."

I cupped both sides of her face. "That part is not happening. We're celebrating you today."

"Miss Hutton, you have a gift that was left at the gate."

Maggie held up an envelope, and Penelope grabbed it from her hand.

"Thank you, Maggie." Penelope flipped the envelope back and forth.

"Open it," Lucy said.

Penelope held the envelope in front of Aspen's face. "Did you send this to me, Aspen?"

"No. Hopefully, it's money."

Everybody gathered around her to watch her peel it open. Penelope's smile slowly faded into shock and worry.

"What is it, baby?" I leaned over her shoulder to scan the letter and saw large letters cut out from newspapers and magazines. *I'm coming for you.*

I snatched the letter from her hands, flipping it back and forth for any clues. "Who dropped off the envelope, Maggie?"

"The guards just handed it to me," Maggie recalled.

I jogged into the house and went to my office and typed on my computer to pull up the security cameras. Bosco and Armani ran in after me a few minutes later.

Bosco asked, "Penelope's crying. What happened?"

I replayed the footage back and watched time stamps to see a young kid on a bike parked in front of my house. He left it with the guard then rode away. Bosco grabbed the phone and dialed security to come in for questioning before I could get a word out.

"Lucinda sent a letter talking about how she's coming for Penelope."

"Lucinda knows where you live?" Armani questioned.

"Hell no, unless we have a mole in security."

A knock brought all our attention in that direction; Donnie stood at the door.

"Boss, you called for me?" Donnie said.

Bosco sat on the edge of the desk and placed the phone on the hook. "What did the delivery kid say to you?"

"Nothing much—except that the package was for Penelope Hutton."

"You check his ID?"

"Yes, and he looked legit."

I stood with my back to him, watching the backyard through the window. Penelope calmed down and talked with her friends.

"What direction or company was he from?"

"He didn't say, and I guess it was the last delivery for him because he said the person was anxious to get it over to her."

My brow lowered at the answer. "Anxious."

"Any other description?" Armani demanded.

"No, I patted him down for any weapons and searched him in the database for any criminal record. It came up solid."

"I have a feeling he might be working with Lucinda to bring you down," Bosco suggested, then he brought the picture up on the screen of the front gate.

"Fuck!"

"Your flight to Chicago can't be changed," Armani informed, then ducked off to the cabinet near the bar and removed a pistol.

"Savio won't take to me canceling last minute." I paced in front of my desk.

Even if our enemies joined forces, I had an army behind me that would take all of them out—along with their bloodlines. Avoiding bringing a war to the city and hearing the Governor's debate on more violence were the least of my worries—but honestly speaking, I had to think about my business first.

"Get someone to sit on the delivery boy, and Bosco you run testing on the note, I mean from the handwriting to the credit card spent on the service."

Bosco left my office, and security stood with Armani.

"Do you want me to go with you to Chicago?"

"I need you here to watch over Penelope."

"She has her own detail; I'm not a babysitter."

"You are now."

Armani grumbled and stomped out of the room.

I sat back in my chair and clicked on the images again to search for any clues. The delivery guy came all the way out to our home on a motorized bike.

My attention lifted toward the knock coming from door. Penelope waltzed in with the rest of the cake in her hand.

"You guys working hard."

Penelope sat down in my lap and scooped some of the cake on the spoon.

I brushed a hand along her back, up to her cheek. "Are you enjoying your party?"

Penelope shoved some in my mouth. "I am, so what made you fly out of there so fast?"

I rubbed a hand up her thigh. "My flight to Chicago was pushed up."

"To when?"

"Now."

Penelope started to rise from my lap. I extended my arm around her waist, urging her to sit back down. "Relax."

"I don't understand how you're going to miss my party. It only happens once."

"Unfortunately, it can't be helped."

Penelope put the plate in her lap. "Tell me the truth. Is something wrong that involves me?"

"The envelope you received; my men are searching for who sent it to my house."

"Are you thinking we were followed?"

I dragged a hand up her back, drew her into a hug. "A possibility."

"Will it affect me going to my internship?"

I strummed my finger on her arm. "I promised to ease up on the extra protection while going out, and I intend to keep it that way."

"Giosuè, are you safe? I mean, you've taken on my burdens."

"Burdens that I would gladly handle until the day I die."

She playfully slapped me on the chest. "You talk like you're okay with dying."

"For you, I will."

She placed the cake on the desk, turned to straddle my lap, and cupped the back of my neck with a caress.

"Even if we never met, I would still belong to you."

I rubbed her back in circular motions, squeezed her to my chest, and kissed her on the cheek.

"We won't let them mess up your party." I knew she should run from me.

Penelope grazed her hand up and down the back of my neck. "I forgot to tell you; I made some friends at the office."

I smacked her on the ass. "Glad you're settling in fine."

She smashed her mouth over mine. "Come on, we have to get back out there."

"I like it just being us here."

"People will wonder what happened."

I hunched my shoulders, slid a hand under her dress, and cupped her ass. "So." My lust for her was timeless and potent.

"Ugh, Giosuè, behave." Penelope crashed a kiss on my lips, sat back to stand, and reached for my hand.

"One drink and then I need to leave for real."

"Anything you say, boss." Penelope giggled, leading me out to the backyard.

Spending time with Penelope for her accomplishments made this even better and watching her walk across that stage for her degree showed how much she wanted to be more than just a girl trying to be on someone's arm. Penelope being on top of her career and not letting me stop her showed she was a bad ass. Either Heath, Alden, or Lucinda tried to stop her progress in life, but she'd put in the work to get what she wanted.

Chapter 15

Penelope

My AirPods lowly buzzed in my ear with Mariah Carey's song, "My All" reminding me of my relationship with Giosuè. My graduation felt like a weight had been lifted, plus my friends loving Giosuè, which made the decision to be with him even more wonderful. In the beginning, I hated him, but then I found out that our backgrounds were similar. We both came from loss, but never let our grief hold us down. He would never admit it but spending time together and physical touch were our love languages. The love of art, and some of the same tastes in food and traveling. Our deep talks and common interests, even with the age difference, felt natural. When he left my bed to fly out to Chicago, I wished I could go, but I knew that leaving a job that I'd just gotten might be frowned upon.

I stapled some paperwork and stacked it in order for my boss to read through. As one of the new interns, I wanted to make a great impression. Agnes had gone above and beyond with helping me learn the ropes. Even some of the other lawyers and assistants had let me sit in a few times when they had to go to a tough judge and research cases.

Agnes was preparing to go take notes from her boss.

"I won't be long. Then we can check the messages and emails."

I put the stapler down and turned in my chair to face her. "I can handle that while you're gone."

"I have about a hundred messages—not to mention emails in the thousands."

"Go and let me do something. When you get back, I will let you know if I have any questions."

"Okay. Anything that sounds like it may be an emergency, set it to the side and come get me." Agnes tapped her palm on the top of my cubicle.

"Gotcha, boss!" I winked.

She laughed and waved me off.

Lunches had become a set thing for our group, and today we were trying a new pizza restaurant that I hadn't been to yet.

Tinsley clicked her nails on the top of my cubicle. "Where's Agnes?"

I glanced up from looking at the papers. "Um, a meeting with her boss."

"How are you doing so far? Run into any tough cases?"

"Not yet."

Tinsley's smile didn't feel genuine. It seemed like she was forcing herself to be nice to me.

"Huh, they have you organizing documents. My first time here I had the Managing Partner's ear and some of the other things, so my time was in the courtroom mostly."

"One day we'll all get lucky."

"Luck? No. It takes more than that to get anywhere in the business."

"How did you get the job again?"

Tinsley pulled on her sleeves of her suit. "Managing Partner is a longtime friend of mine."

"Elio."

"Him, and some other people—but can you do me a favor?" Tinsley held up a stack of papers.

"Depends."

"I mean, you're the intern, so you have to gain some insight, and I need these papers organized, color-coded, and stapled with the signatures highlighted for my boss."

"Can't you do that? As his assistant."

Tinsley snipped, "As the newbie, you should want to help me out. I can put in a good word for you with the bosses."

"Bosses."

Tinsley swished away. "Thanks, Penny."

I yelled to her back. "It's Penelope."

Tinsley threw her hand in the air. "Anyway, see you at lunch."

I slouched back in my chair in a pout. My desk being filled with mountains of documents annoyed me that it would take all day.

"Penelope, are you coming to lunch?" One of the other interns knocked at the edge my cubicle.

I slammed my palm down. "No, I have too much work to do."

"Sorry, you're going to miss out."

"Next time."

After hours and hours of looking at the computer and reading over messages and emails, I made two piles for Agnes to present to her boss: one of emergency files, and others that could be pushed to later. I stretched my arms out wide, yawned, and finally took my eyes off the screen and saw it was dark outside.

The cleaning crew wiped down Agnes's area and smiled at me.

"Eight pm." I turned off my computer and jumped up, grasping my bag to search for my phone. I saw a missed text from Giosuè.

Giosuè: *Don't work too late.*

He sent it around three in the afternoon.

He was still in Chicago. I would have tried to call him, but the day had gone by so fast, causing me to be exhausted. All I wanted was a hot bath and food. So, I sent a text instead.

Me: *Miss you.*

I slid a hand into my jacket and ambled to the elevator, rubbing my eyes. Soon as it came to life I climbed on and clicked for the lobby.

I had slightly closed my eyes when I felt a jolt in the elevator and the lights flickered on and off.

"What the hell?"

It started up again and I relaxed while the numbers slowly fell. Two minutes later, I arrived on the main floor of the building. I strolled out and glanced from left to right, not seeing any security.

I thrusted my arm up to check the time. "Eight fifteen with no security, must be half day or something."

As I headed to the front entrance, I heard the noise of something falling to the ground.

"Is someone there?" My cell buzzed, and I grabbed it out of my pocket.

Unknown: *I've waited a long time for you.*

Frightened at the message and being alone without my security, I replied and jogged away.

Me: *Leave me alone, psycho.*

Unknown: *Do you think your security can save you?*

I gasped at the mention of my security and rushed toward the car parked at the employee section and knocked on the window with no answer. "Hey, let me in."

No one said a word.

I ran to the driver's side and yanked on the door handle —only to find a dead body with a gunshot wound to the head.

"Arghhhhh!"

I stumbled back in shock. Macsen went with Giosuè—even though normally he was with me at all times. I ran across the street to the late-night diner to find some help.

"Help me!"

"Honey, calm down." The waitress stepped before my face, holding menus in her hand.

"You don't understand."

"We're a business. If you have trouble, we can't help you."

"They're dead!"

"Who?"

I put my face into my hands and cried.

"Marie, call the police!" the older waitress yelled.

* * *

I sat on the couch with a blanket around me, around me holding a cup of tea, still frozen from tonight's events.

"Mr. Calabresi's line is still busy. We will continue to try to get through to him."

"Thank you."

At first, Maggie avoided having the police come to the house, but once we informed her that the guards were dead, she allowed them to bring me inside. I still had visions of their dead bodies in my mind.

"Miss Hutton, if you think of anything else, then please let us know." The police officer held a business card in front of me to take.

"She won't be needing that, Officer." Bosco and Armani stood at the entry of the living room.

"Bosco, we're only doing our jobs," the older, gray-haired police officer grumbled.

"My family can take care of Miss Hutton. If she has anything else to say, our attorney will contact you," Bosco announced.

I tucked my feet underneath my legs on the couch.

"If you handle this in any way that ends up with more bodies, then we will have no choice but to bring you both to the station."

"Are you threatening us?" Armani growled, taking a step, and Bosco laid a hand on his shoulder to push him back.

"Barney knows better." Bosco chuckled, coming to stand near me and Maggie.

"I'm fine, officers. Thank you."

Maggie walked them out with Armani trailing behind her with a hand on his holster. Bosco sat on the table and stared at me.

"I will never ask how you're doing. I can tell it was a lot for you to see."

"Have you talked to Giosuè?"

He sighed. "Earlier when I got word about what happened."

I pressed the tissue to my nose. "So, he knows?"

"A little, but he's dealing with some heavy stuff and couldn't get away."

"Is he all right?" I started to jump up from the couch.

"Of course. As soon as he's freed up, he'll be on the earlier flight."

"Thanks for checking on me."

"Can you tell me what happened from the beginning?"

"A typical day that turned to hell."

"Start from the beginning." Bosco held his hands together.

I laid my head on the back of the couch and sighed. "I

had a lot of work today, sifting through messages and emails. I worked late. Then realized I missed lunch and dinner, and finally decided to leave for the day."

"Nobody else was in the building?"

"No—which I guess is normal, but I'm still new."

"My cousin, Elio, has lawyers that work late every week, even debriefing on the weekends," Bosco said.

"This was intentional."

"Not necessarily.My family vets everyone that works for us."

"So, an outside person?"

"Maybe. I need to get the footage or talk with Elio. Most of the security that works in front were off or together in the breakroom."

"I don't want anyone to be fired."

"That's the least of their worries."

I gulped at this statement. "Are you saying he's going to kill the security guards?"

"The less you know the better."

"Bosco, you have to promise me that Elio and Giosuè won't kill innocent people. It wasn't their fault."

"I'd be the last person to lie to you, Penelope. Your best bet is to talk to Giosuè."

"While he's away, as the underboss, you can make decisions."

His brows fell into a frown. "You know a lot about my job. Should I be worried about that, Little Dove?"

"Bosco."

Bosco stood from the table. "The decision is already made."

"Please, talk to your brother. I never ask for anything, but enough killing has gone on."

"Run down what happened after you got on the elevator; my source said the lights flickered."

I moved my hand up and down. "Yeah, and kind of jolted like it stopped moving for a minute."

Bosco rubbed his chin. "Someone tampered with the elevator."

"I think so. A minute later it started up again and I got off in the lobby."

"Did something else happen out of the blue?"

Recalling the text messages, I reached for my purse, grabbed my phone, and held it out for him.

"Text messages and I heard a bang."

"A banging sound?"

"Like someone dropped something."

Bosco scrolled in my phone and read off the text messages. "Does my brother know about these messages?"

"Yes."

"Okay, get some rest, and I will check on you in the morning."

"When is Giosuè coming home?"

"Soon. Remember the police can't help you. Anything else happens call me or Armani."

"Armani hates me."

"Armani hates everyone." Bosco chuckled, then left the living room.

I laid back down and covered myself in the wool blanket, preparing to dial Giosuè's number again when another text message popped up.

Unknown: *Next time, Little Dove.*

I leaped off the couch, dropped the phone on the floor, and curled up in the corner in fear. Maggie rushed in and held her arms out for me. "Miss Hutton, are you okay?"

Bosco was surprisingly still there, and he popped in with a gun in his hand. "What happened?"

"Pho-on-phone."

Bosco bent down and picked it up, narrowing his brows in anger. "Who all knows you by that name?"

"Giosuè and you guys. Is he—"

"Is he what?"

I raised my hand to wipe a tear off my cheek. "Call him for me."

"He's busy, Penelope. My guys are working on tracking the number."

"Giosuè—I want to talk to Giosuè, *now!*"

Bosco nodded, removing another phone from his shoulder pocket and making a call.

"Is he around?" Bosco asked.

Maggie and I watched him turn to whisper lowly, "Get him on the phone."

"I want to go to Chicago," I pleaded.

He sighed. "You can't."

"Why not?"

"Because he doesn't need distractions right now."

"That's funny, me beng a distraction for him." I marched out of the living room and jogged upstairs to my bedroom, then slammed the door.

"He's on his way!" Bosco yelled, from downstairs.

"My life is a mess." I groaned.

* * *

I guess Bosco was able to get Giosue' back on a flight immediately because it felt like I hadn't slept for too long after last night's events. I didn't get to feel his touch that was soothing. The sound of his voice affected me deeply. My insides rippled with excitement feeling his long tongue latch on to my right breast. Each time I saw him the pull was stronger, like drowning under his gaze, making sure he never wanted love from anyone besides me. Water pelted along our skin in the shower. Emotions melted to resolve that being kidnapped started as me hating him, but now I never wanted to leave. His dick's invitation was a passionate challenge, hard to resist and automatically opened up to allow free rein.

Giosuè's sheer masculinity overwhelmed me. "You're going to make them think I'm hurting you."

"It hurts so good..." I moaned and brushed a hand down his back. He pushed forward and bit down on my shoulder and I squeezed my eyes shut.

"Fuck, baby!" His thrusts got more and more aggressive.

Giosuè palmed my breasts, licking across each nipple.

I gasped as he pushed his finger into my behind. "Oh, God, let's take it to the bedroom."

"Can I have you always?"

I licked him like a cat. "Always. Never leave me."

He moved back slowly, dick sticking out straight with our combined cream. He reached to turn the knob on the faucet. I climbed out of the tub to take a towel, and he tossed it on the floor, smacking me on the ass.

"Bed now."

I switched out of the bathroom and left a trail of water on the floor. I made a mental note to clean up—otherwise, we'd slip and fall. I climbed up onto the bed, lying flat on my back with my legs spread wide. I ran a hand down my chest, spreading my lower lips.

"Come taste your favorite sweets."

Giosuè hadn't taken me to his playroom in a while, and I hoped we'd have a chance to explore more of his toys. My eagerness excited him when I exerted dominance, but then he'd take it back in a flash—like right now, he stalked over to the side of the bed and pulled open the nightstand drawer, taking out a bottle of lube and a vibrator, and sat on the bed.

"I'm in charge."

"Yes, sir."

He carefully poured the liquid around his thick shaft, turned the vibrator on, placed it on my ass, and slowly pressed it into my entryway with his dick on my pussy.

"Giosuè! So much at once."

"Keep taking us, baby."

I curved my palms around the sheets, my legs bouncing on the top of the comforter. My head fell back, and my voice went silent.

"Kiss me." Everything was perfect now.

His kisses were cruel, devouring my will to resist.

"You look so beautiful, Little Dove. All this belongs to me."

I swallowed the lump in my throat. My legs tingled when he pressed an inch further, making me aware of the sensual experience we shared. I felt heavy and warm. "Please. I want you."

"Fuck, I can't wait any longer." Giosuè tossed the vibrator to the side and pushed my legs backwards, thrusting in and out.

At his age, his virility captivated me with how much I could learn. He was so compelling, potent in his moves from slow to fast, hitting my spots. A hot ache grew in my chest, and I thrusted my tongue out and captured his lips. My fingers caressed his chest. Swinging us around with me on top, Giosuè locked his hands on my hips, thrusting from the bottom. I pressed my feet flat against the mattress and rocked up and down.

"Close your eyes," he whispered.

I fluttered my eyes and bounced faster, moaning.

"We're on an island, just the two of us."

I gripped his biceps. "Yes…"

Softly his breath shifted in a low groan. "I'm fucking you in the water, your screams only for me to hear. Do you know why?"

"Yes, because you—"

He was my every hope and fantasy.

"Tell me what we already know, beautiful."

"I'm yours."

"Mine!" He leaned forward, kissing me slowly and thoughtfully, dragging kisses down my chest and leaving my body burning with fire. He devoured me at every stroke. I came, shaking, eyes rolling in the back of my head.

"Come with me."

"Mmmmmhhhmmm…my favorite part."

* * *

"Have you spoken to any of the security team at the office?"

Giosuè poured more coffee in his cup and took a sip, leaning back in his chair on the patio as we ate breakfast.

The night of the incident I barely slept from missing him and fearing the person would come back to the office and hurt me again. Giosuè not answering my calls angered me, but eventually—with a lot of apologies and making up—

we came to an agreement. He would make sure to answer me—unless it was a dire situation.

"Elio and Armani questioned the entire staff and we watched footage from the lobby."

"Did you catch the person? What about the outside cameras?"

"They were good to cover themselves, but are you okay with going back today?"

I bit into my toast with butter and wiped my mouth on my napkin.

"If Macsen is there, I will feel better."

Giosuè stretched his palm across the table, covering my hand. "Even if a bug gets too close, let me know and I will kill them."

I smirked. "A bug."

"A smile is what I'm after."

"You've put a lot of smiles on my face lately, but a few times I did frown."

He leaned forward and crashed his mouth onto mine. "I apologize again, Little Dove."

"I forgive you."

Chapter 16

Giosuè

Savio watched his children play on the swings in the park, while we were parked a few feet away. Their nanny and his wife managed to keep the kids from running off like they normally did, and I was impressed at how my cousin had settled into fatherhood. The darkened SUV stopped, and I unbuttoned my coat and waited for him to speak.

"A mess is brewing in New York," Savio said. He lifted a briefcase on his lap, popped it open, and took out a manila envelope.

"A problem I have to end soon."

"Money is being interrupted because of your problems, cousin."

I turned my head to look at him. "What are you saying?"

"Elio or I never get involved in deals you manage, but do you not agree it has gotten out of hand?" Savio gestured to the photos of Matevi meeting with a few of Paraskeva's people.

I clenched and unclenched my fist. "No more than what you have seen before, let alone your other brother's."

"On my end, I have it all under control. Bulgarians aren't likely to get out of hand."

"How committed are you when you're mixing business and pleasure?"

"Money is flowing through the art gallery and the ports, gun sales are up ten percent, and I run my business how I see fit." I turned my body to face him.

"Lucky you are family. Iit's the only time I allow disrespect."

"I am not your little brothers."

Savio grinned. "Armani told me you're in love."

"Are we here to talk business or not?"

Savio waved a hand at me. "Business, cousin—but we heard of some problems with her being stalked."

"Not for long. Lucinda is pissed I took her prized possession."

"Listen you can take my advice or not. Everything happens for a reason. Protect her at all costs by keeping her informed or you will lose everything."

I agreed, flipping over the old pictures of Lucinda and Penelope at the mansion.

"Funds are moving nicely; even offshore accounts have tripled."

"Bring your woman to meet the family."

Our attention went to my cell blasting. Bosco knew I would be caught up and not able to talk.

"We should go to the house and finish discussing what should happen next for Lucinda."

Savio answered his phone at the same time as I checked mine. The kids ran back to the car with his wife and nanny, laughing.

Bosco: *Situation at home.*
Me: *Something you can handle?*
Bosco: *Penelope got attacked.*

The car pulled into traffic, heading toward their home.

Me: *Where is she?*
Bosco: *Home, guards were killed.*
Me: *I'm coming home.*

Savio whipped around, kissed Mckayla, and dragged out his conversation. The car came up to his parents' compound.

"I got the call already. The flight is gassing up for you to fly back out." Savio climbed out, then helped his wife and son.

"Uncle and Aunt, nice to see you both."

"I find out you are dating a young woman from my boys and not you." Uncle Elio playfully smacked me on the cheek.

"You will meet her soon. I promise, Uncle."

Savio's mother stretched her arms wide for a hug, making me bend down closer to her height to make it easier.

"Giosuè has to fly out for an emergency, but he will bring her by soon," Savio told them, removed his coat, and pushed it into the house manager's arms.

* * *

As soon as my flight got back from Chicago, and I crawled into bed with Penelope, I could feel her clinging to me in fear. Most times Bosco and Armani would be with me on a trip to Chicago but Penelope's protection was more important. They were both equipped to deal with any problems if I wasn't around.

It going on one am in the neighborhood where Lucinda was working with Paraskeva kind of benefitted me in the long run. I slipped the black gloves on and folded down my mask. Armani nodded. Time to make our presence known. I twisted the silencer on tight, jumping out of the back of the car. I trekked up to the guard and placed my hand around his mouth. "If you keep your mouth closed and do as I say, I might let you live."

He nodded and dropped the gun from his hands. I kicked it out of the way. Armani snatched it up and motioned for the team to move forward.

"Split right and left. Bosco take the rear," Armani demanded.

"We only have five minutes before they change staff."

I shoved his guard forward to step up and knock on the door. "Remember I will kill you if you give away anything."

He slowly knocked after I removed my hand.

"What!"

"Open up. I need to pee." Looking at me from the corner of his eye, he nervously fumbled with his hands. I put a finger to my lips for him to be quiet. Right as the door opened, I forcefully shoved him into the other bodyguard and sent a shot into the one sitting on the loveseat.

"Where is Lucinda?"

"Fuck you!"

Pop! Pop!

"Arghhhh!" He fell to the floor after I shot him twice in both arms.

"Where is Lucinda?"

"Help me! Do you know who I am?" A loud shriek from upstairs caught my attention.

"Please let me go," the guard cried, begging on the ground. Armani kicked him in the face, picked up his gun, and shot him in the head.

Bosco and a few of our men came from the back. Lucinda dragged her feet downstairs and stopped in the middle of the floor.

"Lucinda, nice to see you again."

"Giosuè, we can work together. I know a lot of secrets that can help you."

I marched to the middle of the floor, pushed the gun under her chin, and lifted her head. Tears trickled down her cheeks.

"Let her go!" Loud shouting and tussling from the hall drew my focus.

"He is trying to take my gun," one of my men stated, then knocked her personal bodyguard on the head with the muzzle of his gun.

"Lucinda, you've wasted a lot of my time and money, sending your men to stalk my woman, only to end up back where you started on your knees." I seethed through my teeth.

"All right, Giosuè, we can make a deal; I will leave the country."

"Shit, you had the chance, but ended up here in Philadelphia, scheming with Paraskeva to get my ports and hurt the people I love."

"I had no choice!" Lucinda spat.

"You always have a choice."

Lucinda lifted her palm to smack me, and I captured her wrist and squeezed. "One raised hand equals one life." I stared at her and pointed my gun at her boytoy and shot him in the center of his chest.

Lucinda reached to crawl to him, and I snatched her back. "No! You bastard."

"Take her with us."

"The rest of the bodies?"

"Get the acid."

As we walked out of the home, the ringing of my phone piqued my interest. "What do you have for me?"

"Come to the warehouse."

"On the way."

Little Dove: *Why am I sleeping alone?*
Me: *Not for too much longer.*
Little Dove: *Hurry up.*
Me: *I love you.*
Little Dove: *Love you too.*

Speeding back to the plane, we blew through red lights, even with the empty streets of Philly. I had to call and thank my cousin for delivering the photos and information to the address of the house. The house being tucked out in a small area with barely any residents made it easier to get in and not be noticed. Bosco tapped away on his phone, turning it to show me confirmation of the bodies being dragged out in body bags.

"Make sure there are no traces."

"On it," Bosco answered.

Armani sat across from us, checked his gun, and put it back in the holster. "Paraskeva won't be easy."

"I know."

We crossed over the freeway to the private jet airport and jumped out, bringing a handcuffed Lucinda on the flight to sit next to Armani and two armed soldiers.

"Penelope won't be safe just because I'm dead," Lucinda warned.

I picked up the bottle of Dom Perignon and poured a glass. "Put a muzzle on her."

Lucinda laughed and squirmed in her seat when the cloth came over her mouth. The seatbelt sign came on and I rested near the exit with my head laid back, eyes closed.

"You're worried."

I popped my left eye wide at Bosco talking to me. "I'm good."

"Coverage is tripled at the house."

"I know." I reached for my cell, logging into the security cameras from the app.

* * *

The need to be in bed with Penelope and let my brothers handle killing Lucinda started to ramp up the longer it took to get her chained up to the wall. All she did was cry and threaten my men if she wasn't released.

My brother tapped me on the shoulder to look over at our guests. "What do you have for me?"

"Paraskeva and Bozhidarov are locked in my trunk," Tinsley explained. Many times, I would succumb to her biting her bottom lip when she was between my legs, but we had business to handle.

"How did you manage to grab them both together?"

"A little extra topping in their drinks."

Tinsley stuck her hand in her bra and pulled out a small bottle filled with liquid.

"Drugged them."

"Enough to fall asleep for a minute."

"Bring them in here." I snapped my finger.

Tinsley stood on her tiptoes and leaned in to kiss me on the mouth. I jerked back.

I slapped her hand down. "Act accordingly."

"Ever since you got a little girlfriend, you've changed."

"Jealous?"

"Of her, never." Tinsley grabbed her gun, and I blocked her hand from pointing it at Lucinda.

I gazed in her eyes for any hesitancy. "We have a problem."

Tinsley mumbled low, "I know my place."

"Then you should remember it's safer for you to be what I want—and that's my solider."

"Understood."

A few minutes passed by, and I released her hand as Armani dumped them on the floor. "We seemed to come across an unfortunate situation, gentlemen. It could have been a great working relationship if you took my offer."

I slouched down and watched each man. Paraskeva burst into laughter and his underboss looked off. I trailed his eye movement to a window up high in the right corner.

"Should have known you would do something stupid," Paraskeva said.

A loud horn got our attention. All my men got in position with their guns when a blast happened that threw me back against the wall. Bullets started flying everywhere. There were loud screams, yelling, and then silence rang in my ear. I slowly scooted to the back of the hallway and grasped the doorknob to stand when another blast came from the back door. I locked my gun on the first person I saw and shot him.

Bosco ran up to me, shooting at another Bulgarian cartel. "We have to go!"

I drew Bosco close. "Armani, where's Armani."

"Right here!" Armani rushed over to my sore right side to help walk me out.

"Shit, are they dead?"

"I got them." Bosco spoke.

"I want to see."

"We have no time," Bosco grumbled. I jerked away to go back inside, and he pushed back for me to get in the car. Macsen stood on the side of the trunk with an automatic AK, killing the people on the top of the building.

"He set us up."

"Let's go!" Armani shouted, slapping the back of the seat. Macsen hopped in the passenger seat as the car drove away.

Bosco lifted my shirt, checked for any wounds.

I winced, holding my right side. "I'm good, just sore."

"Tinsley! Did she get out?" Armani searched for her.

"Fuck! Let me try to call her." I started to dial her number when it rang.

"Are you all right?" Tinsley screamed.

I snapped my fingers for everyone to stop talking. "Where are you?"

"Heading home," Tinsley replied.

"Keep the lines clear until we get confirmation they're dead."

Our presence was too hot at the moment; we couldn't wait any longer to get away.

"Giosuè."

"What?"

Tinsley hesitated. "I—"

"What Tinsley?"

"Nothing." She exhaled a breath.

Tinsley's dial tone beeped in when another call popped up.

Macsen leaned in the seat as we descended from the area, only to see road and trees. "I have the computer footage of the warehouse. Police got called."

"Shit."

"Had to be Tinsley."

"Yeah, she probably did it to make sure we're not seen as the aggressive one."

"Get Foster on the line to confirm the deaths and call Savio."

"Elio is texting me now." Armani answered his phone.

"Macsen, I want you to come back out here with the lawyer to make sure any questions get pushed off on the Bulgarians. Make it look like they staged it to blame it on us."

"He's right here." Armani held the phone for me to talk.

"Elio," I answered.

"Savio is on the line," Elio said.

"Everybody safe?" Savio inquired.

"We are."

"Stick by home for the next few days," Savio stated.

"I agree," Elio agreed.

I scrubbed a hand over my face. "Already on my mind. Penelope and I were going to come out to Chicago to visit."

"Let the smoke clear and then fly out," Savio advised.

Stretched back in the seat, I shut my eyes, arms crossed in thought, as my phone buzzed. Seeing Agent Foster's name, I placed the phone to my ear and answered. Streetlights sheltered us through the darkness as the New York streets appeared.

"There are helicopters and police all over the area!" DEA Agent Foster shouted.

We finally curved off the freeway to the main road. The gates split for us to pull in. Extra security was standing at each corner with automatic weapons. I clicked and put him on mute, slid from the seat, moved around, and waved for a few guards to come to me.

"Bosco, we need to make sure people are covered at the art gallery, office, and clubs."

"Taken care of soon as we drove here." Bosco jogged upstairs, and I trailed him.

I unmuted and put Foster on speaker.

"You need to make sure nothing goes wrong," I explained.

"Already on top of things, but it's a lot, Giosuè," Foster replied.

"Don't let me down." I disconnected the call.

I pushed a hand in my pocket and marched in to see Maggie and Albe, standing and whispering in the corner. They pulled apart and strolled up to me.

"Mr. Calabresi, we heard on the news that there was an explosion at one of your businesses."

In confusion, my brows lowered together. I slipped out of my jacket and heard yelling from the kitchen. "Where's Penelope?"

"Bedroom," Maggie answered.

"Are we on lockdown?" Abel checked.

Bosco came out of the kitchen. "They hit the gallery."

"I need to check on Penelope. Meet me in my office."

I rushed upstairs and busted into her room, finding her curled up under the covers. I released a long-held breath, shut the door, and stared at her for a long minute. My life really changed after seeing her for the first time. The harder I worked, the better I felt about her being in my world.

For an hour, I kept watch over her until my eyes started to drift closed. I got up and headed to my bedroom and prepared for bed.

Chapter 17

Penelope

I rolled onto my back, and my eyes slowly fluttered open. I glanced to side of the bed that Giosuè usually slept in, but it was completely empty. I rubbed my hand over my eyes and scooted up against the headboard. I extended my hand to the left of the bed to check the time, threw the covers off my legs, and rose from the bed. Only wearing a pair of panties and a bra, I picked up my robe, trekked to the bathroom, and scanned to see if Giosuè was there.

"It's eight in the morning," I mumbled to myself, walking from my bedroom down the hall, then downstairs to the kitchen, where I saw only Maggie.

"Morning, Miss Hutton."

"Morning. Have you seen Giosuè?"

"He had to take of business earlier than expected," Maggie explained.

"So, he came home."

Maggie and the housekeeper made eye contact. "He wanted me to tell you to not worry."

I had no right to be mad at her, so I just smiled and turned to head upstairs to change clothes.

"Will you have your usual meal?" Maggie asked.

"No, I have to get to the office today."

"Is that wise with everything going on?"

I paused, then swiveled my head to the side. "Giosuè put extra men on my detail. I will be fine."

"Yes, ma'am."

I placed a hand on her shoulder. "Maggie please call me Penelope."

"Yes, Penelope." Maggie patted my hand.

I made it to the bedroom, shut and locked the door, then lifted a pillow and screamed out my frustrations. There was always so much talking, but he was still leaving me out of all the discussions—especially when it was about my life.

Already annoyed with him and with my stomach growling, I stomped to the closet and settled on pants, a long black shirt and blazer. I started the shower and put the clothes on the bed next to some underwear. After looking for any messages from Giosuè, I hopped in the shower, standing with my back against the water, and let the kinks work through as I washed.

* * *

Forty-five minutes later, I stepped into the office to see people working. Some of them looked somber and were crying.

"Agnes, what's going on?"

Agnes stood at the receptionist's desk with folders in her hands. "A fire happened at Elio's cousin's gallery."

I reared back, thinking of Giosuè. "Art gallery?"

Agnes nodded, gripping my hand and pulling me into

the empty conference room. She shut the door and closed the blinds. "Allegedly, a war broke out with the Calabresi and Bulgarian cartels."

I gulped. "You know about the Calabresi cartel?"

"I might work in a law firm, but I know everything about that part of Elio's life."

"Right, yeah." I cleared my throat.

"How are you doing? After everything that went down here."

"Um, okay. Giosuè wanted me to stay away from here, but putting my life on hold will only mean they won."

"No idea who tried to kill you?"

I slouched in my chair. "None."

"Well, you're more than welcome to stay with me if that big mansion gets to be lonely," Agnes joked.

I grinned at her comment. "Thank you, but Giosuè has it handled."

Agnes arched her left brow, turned, and led us from the conference room. I bumped into a soft body.

"Penelope, you okay?" Tinsley asked.

"Ugh."

"Penelope." Agnes snapped her fingers in my face.

"Sorry, tired brain."

"Agnes working you too hard?" Tinsley chuckled.

Agnes waved her off and ambled down the hall. I took a seat, turned on my computer, and placed my purse in my cabinet. Once again, I scanned my threads to see if there was anything from Giosuè.

A silent vibration knocked me out of my trance of reading over emails, and I answered my phone.

His deep voice evoked a tremble in my panties. "Little Dove."

"Giosuè."

"Before you start, let me explain."

I sat back in my chair. "Oh, I'd love to hear you explain."

"I came home, it was late, and I kissed you on the cheek, but you were deep in sleep and I hated to ruin it with worry."

I pushed up to my desk and placed an elbow on top. "Let me make that decision. Where are you?"

"On the way home."

"For how long?"

"My cousins want me to bring you to Chicago." He changed the subject.

"So, I'm meeting the rest of the family now?" I teased.

He chuckled. "You are."

I twirled a finger around my ponytail. "So, I must be important to you."

"More than important."

"Well, you can make up for your mishap by letting my friends come over for dinner."

He groaned. "Dinner?"

"Yes, some girls from work and my friends from school." I clicked on my computer, scrolling through messages.

"Fine, but I expect you to be naked in the playroom tonight."

"I was naked last night."

"You had on a bra and panties."

"I can make that happen." I giggled and crossed my legs.

"I like my odds."

"Me too." I blushed, scratching the top of my hand.

The phone went silent, each of us listening to the other breathe.

"If anything happens, you have men everywhere on the floor and outside."

I glanced into the corner at the undercover security guard. He dipped his head at me. "That's my security?"

"Not taking chances."

"See you tonight."

I dropped the call and swiped through papers on my desk in a daze, thinking about how the night would go with Giosuè.

* * *

Agnes couldn't wait to come to the house and see how the other half lived. I kept telling her that I was working class like her, and Giosuè was the one with money. Maggie let me organize the meal plan for tonight when I called earlier to make plans. Aspen and Lucy even asked to bring something, but I declined.

"Hey now, that kiss is doing something to me."

"Good."

"Giosuè, we have guests coming, and you promised to wait until after dinner. Plus, I want to talk about what happened with the art gallery."

Giosuè removed his arms from around my waist, stepped back, reached for my wrist, and turned me around to talk face-to-face.

Giosuè clasped our hands together. "I apologize for not waking you last night."

"Tell me what happened. Don't leave anything out."

"We were set up after we got to Lucinda."

"By who?"

"Who do you think?"

I hiked a brow. "Lucinda."

Killing someone was never in my bones, but that woman continued to turn my life upside down and I wished to be rid of her forever. The doorbell let me know that my guests had arrived. I laid a hand on Giosuè's chest and pecked him on the lips.

"We can talk more later."

"Who all did you invite?"

"Just a few girls from work and your brother." I grinned at him, and he shook his head.

Armani walked in behind Lucy and Aspen giving their coats to Maggie. I let Giosuè's hand go and ran to my girls.

"Babe, you look gorgeous," Aspen screeched, giving me air kisses.

Bosco trekked in next before the door closed and pinched me on the cheek, I slapped his hand down.

"Lucy, Aspen, you remember Giosuè's brothers." I shifted around them and answered the doorbell to see Agnes and Brittney.

"Thanks for coming."

Agnes stuck out a bottle of champagne at me. "Your home is beautiful." Abel helped all the girls remove their coats.

"I told you not to bring anything."

Agnes shrugged. "Elio said he's going to be a little late."

Giosuè stood, talking with his brothers.

"Come on, the food will be ready soon. Brittney, you met my best friends at lunch, right?"

Brittney smiled at them.

Maggie stepped in the hallway. "Dinner will be served in five minutes if you and your guests want to come in the dining room."

"Come on. Armani, I suggest you behave tonight."

I caught him staring at Brittney's ass.

Giosuè caught his arm around my neck and pressed a

kiss on my forehead. "You have one hour for the dinner, then it's my time."

"Nope, you made me suffer, so you can hang for a few hours." I clapped him on the shoulder.

All the girls sat down, with Armani next to Brittney, and Giosuè and Bosco at each head of the table. Lisa poured each of us a glass of champagne. I took a sip, feeling the bubbly tickle my stomach.

As the food started to be served, I heard the doorbell ring and stood. Giosuè captured my hand.

"Where are you going?"

"To grab the door."

"I have people for that."

I placed a hand on my hip. "It's another guest."

"Who?"

"Drink and be nice while I'm gone."

Aspen and the rest of the girls giggled at my response. Before I could make it out of the dining room, Maggie and Tinsley appeared.

"Fuck."

Giosuè cursed, and I whipped around at the anger in his facial features. Tinsley sauntered in farther. I reached her and clasped her hand to show her to the table.

"Tinsley, you know the girls already, but I wanted you to meet my boyfriend and his brothers."

"Armani and Bosco, we've already met," Tinsley said.

I paused at her admission, looking from the glare on her face to Giosuè.

"Dinner is lamb chops, spinach, rice, and salad," Maggie announced, leaving us alone.

I motioned between the two. "Do you two know each other?" That same odd feeling creeped up again.

Tinsley smirked and sat down.

"You need to leave." Giosuè pushed his chair back and jumped up.

"I invited her to dinner."

Tinsley licked her lips. "Giosuè, is that any way to talk to one of your favorite girls?"

"Wait, you two know each other." I motioned between Tinsley and Giosuè.

"Tinsley, you need to leave," Bosco demanded.

"Someone needs to answer me!" I shouted.

Giosuè snatched me by the arm and dragged me out of the room to the hallway. Giosuè pleaded, "Tinsley is no one to me."

I held a hand in the air. "She works with me."

"At the law firm?"

I nodded and watched the color drain from Giosuè's face. "I think I'm going to be sick."

"Look, I will kick her out." Giosuè smashed our mouths together, then pulled back and rubbed my lower back.

Agnes, Brittney, and the rest of the girls came into the entryway. "We're going to go and let you two talk."

"Yeah, Penelope, I think you two should fire that girl. I always had a bad feeling about her."

"Thanks guys, but we can finish dinner. I really wanted you all to meet. Let me go freshen my face and I will be brand new." I hugged Aspen.

Everyone went back in to sit down, and I inched to the bathroom in Giosuè's office. I twisted the faucet to a cool temperature, moving a towel underneath the flow to wash my face. As soon as the cool towel hit my forehead, I felt replenished, tossed it back on the counter, ready to head back to dinner when the doorknob jiggled, and Tinsley came inside.

"What are you doing?"

"Giosuè wants me to leave."

"If I knew you and him had a relationship, I would have never asked you to come tonight. Why'd you let me talk about him at work?"

Tinsley hissed. "You're so naive."

I reared my head back. "Naïve?"

Tinsley pulled a gun out of her pocket and held it at her side.

I gasped in surprise. "Tinsley!"

Tinsley yanked on my arm. "Keep your mouth shut and come with me."

"No." I jerked out of her grip.

"I suggest you come with me now, before I really hurt you and everybody here." Tinsley waved the gun in the air, then looked over her shoulder.

I covered my mouth in awareness of the past shooting at the office. "It was your perfume."

Tinsley gloated. "Fun fact: Giosuè bought that perfume for me."

I stepped forward and lunged with my arms up, and she quickly cocked back the safety on her weapon. We stumbled out of the bathroom to the hallway.

"Try it and see what happens. Giosuè is mine. As soon as you came along, he tossed me to the side like I meant nothing," Tinsley argued, eyes moving back and forth.

I thought back to the office when I would brag about Giosuè, and I felt like she was probably sad about not having someone. I realized she wanted my life, and the man that I had come to love. Tinsley waved the gun in my face to start moving, when out the corner of my eye, Lucy came in view on my left side.

"Arhhhh!" Lucy started to run off, but Tinsley pointed her gun between the both of us.

Tinsley snatched me by the arm. Lucy's scream pulled the rest of the dinner party's attention to us.

"That night I almost had you. Those sorry worthless guards had no clue when I came up to the car thinking I only wanted to talk, then their eyes ballooned at me pulling my gun out."

"At the time I had no clue if the scent lingered."

Tinsley sneered and shoved the gun in my face. "Connect the dots and you'd realize it was me the entire time."

I exhaled a breath as Giosue' slowly approached us.

"Giosuè." I whispered.

"Tinsley, you've been stalking Penelope."

Tinsley growled. "She doesn't deserve you. I've put in the time and work to be everything you needed, baby."

"Tinsley, you work for the family. I always told you our relationship was strictly business."

"Because you never gave me a chance." Tinsley gripped the back of my hair tighter and nudged the gun into my cheek.

Giosuè raised both hands in the air. "Take me instead and we can talk about you and me."

Tinsley chuckled. "He thinks I'm stupid. I bet you never told her I'm one of the hitmen for the Calabresi cartel. If someone is marked for death, then they call me."

Giosuè's facial expression showed that he was irritated with the conversation.

"So many times, we'd be up in the air, and my lips would be around his thick pole," Tinsley taunted, kicking the back door open and dragging me back.

My friends all stood in shock. Armani and Bosco slowly came up on either side of Giosuè. Tinsley glanced to the right then left at the guards with loaded guns.

"Call off your soldiers or she's dead."

"Stand down," Giosuè demanded.

"He's never going to be with you, Tinsley, even if I'm dead."

"Shut up!" Tinsley screamed.

Giosuè winked at me and charged at us. I shook my head and watched in horror as Tinsley raised the gun in his direction.

"Stop or I'm going to kill you!" Tinsley shouted and pulled the trigger.

I watched Giosuè's body jerk back in pain. Anger took over me, and I tossed my head back, knocked her in the chin, and started to turn to fight back.

"Penelope, get down!" Armani yelled.

Giosuè jumped on top of me as bullets riddled Tinsley's body. Giosuè slowly rolled over, blood spilling from his mouth.

"Giosuè, stay with me. Help is coming," I begged while covering his bullet wound with my hand.

Bosco and Armani sprinted to their brother, ripped his suit jacket apart, and tied a piece of his shirt around his wound to slow the bleeding. Ambulance and police sirens blasted nearby, and I prayed that Giosuè would be fine—even with the faraway look in his eyes.

Chapter 18

Giosuè

A year ago, I would have never expected to be living with a woman, let alone jumping in front of a bullet to save her—unless it was my mother or another family member. Penelope stuck by me through my recovery and even my stubbornness of not wanting her help. The bullet went in and out, with no long-term damage. I still had to listen to her and Maggie complaining about me working too much right after I got the approval from the doctor to go back to work. Armani warmed up to Penelope during the entire process and even took her side—especially at moments when I winced from overexerting myself. Even getting Penelope to leave the house was a task within itself because she was scared from my shooting, but her friends wanted to hang out. I sent her in a brand-new Lamborghini, with her own credit card to spoil herself. Protection around the clock never stopped— even with some of my enemies buried.

"How do you see the coverup for a major cartel leader being dead in your factory?" DEA Agent Foster pushed forward in the chair inside my office. I put off our meetings for weeks, not ready to hear him bitching about having to split his money with other counterparts.

I flipped through the pile of pictures from the police report. "Factory was sold months ago."

"Giosuè, we both know you had those papers doctored to look like it was sold."

"Do you have proof?"

He lowered his eyes to the ground.

"Then I suggest you come up with something else. If you would have taken certain conversations more seriously when I presented them, we'd have no problems. Don't you think?" I pushed the direction of the conversation to imply if he had been serious about his money, Bulgarians being in New York wouldn't be his fault.

"Police files only disappear if I can make a deal happen."

"Foster, they will go missing whether you are in the middle or not. Certainly, you would not have me put my family at risk?"

"No, I meant—"

"I know what you meant, and I sympathize, but there are more important matters to handle."

"Like what?"

"More expansion on the docks, and the art gallery is getting rebuilt from the mess of the fire that you should have prevented."

"Come on. You know that was out of my hands."

"Again, I pay you a nice fee and I still come out on the short end of the stick."

Agent Foster hopped up, shaking his head. "How much are you talking?"

"Enough that regulation is not in my way. Inspections

will not be tripled in costs, and construction is handled without any problems from your people."

"Giosuè, I will make it work. No more blowing up buildings or trafficking through the union's trucking companies."

"Long as I have more ports, we can live without the garbage trucks. Besides, my brother is thinking about starting a trucking company."

"Transporting across state lines."

"If that's his decision, I can count on your support?" I questioned.

His face looked void of any emotions. "Sure, Giosuè."

I stood, extending my hand. "Thank you, Governor. Cheer up, your wife and kids will love riding on the private yacht I gifted you." I smirked.

* * *

I packed my bags last night before I went to bed and ordered the jet to be filled and ready for our trip to Chicago. Penelope was still out with her friends and coming straight to the airport when they finished. Bosco and Armani sat in their seats on the plane, talking and jabbing each other like little kids again.

"If you two continue, I will put you both in time out."

They flipped me off at the same time.

"When is Penelope coming?" Armani checked.

"She's twenty minutes away."

"How did everything pan out with Foster down your back?"

I clung to my phone, reviewing messages. "It went as expected. He's going to take the money that we give him and shut up."

"He better."

"Oh, I gave him your yacht as a gift." I pointed at Armani.

"What!" Armani started to jump out of his seat, forgetting he was buckled up.

Bosco and I chuckled.

"Family first."

"Fuck the family." Armani's nostrils flared.

A loud horn stopped my next words and I caught sight of Penelope's car pulling up to the gate.

"She's coming."

"Penelope still okay with everything?" Bosco prodded.

"Are you asking have we talked about Tinsley since the incident?"

Bosco took a sip of his drink. "Yep."

"Not yet. I think Chicago is the best place to relax, have her around more family before we go deeper into my personal affairs."

"Tinsley was a wrong move," Bosco reminded me.

I sighed. "I know, so stop bringing it up. At first, she understood that it was a sexual relationship only."

"She's a woman," Bosco said, taking his ringing phone out to answer.

I jumped up to aid Penelope as she entered the plane and took her bag, kissing her on the lips.

"You look glowing."

"Spa day."

"Fuck!" Bosco shouted, hitting his hand on the side of the seat.

"What's the matter?"

His eyes went up to Penelope, then back to me and nodded.

"You can talk business, Bosco. I am no longer a naive

college student." Penelope took a seat across from me and brought out her AirPods.

"We'll have a conversation when we get to Chicago," Bosco said.

"How bad is it?"

"Bad enough that we might need backup," Bosco replied.

The pilot came on the intercom to give directions. The flight attendant shut the doors. I reached for Little Dove's hand and kissed the back of her palm. Business would wait until we settled in Chicago and got around family. I finished the rest of my drink and slowly rested my eyes to clear my head from all the bullshit with Tinsley and Lucinda.

As soon as the flight ended, I had soldiers lined up, ready to escort us to my uncle Elio's home. Savio wanted to meet there—even though we'd be staying with his family while we were in town.

Penelope shuffled beside me as I helped her off the jet and to the blacked-out Rolls Royce. Bosco and Armani hopped in the other bulletproof Phantom, trailing along.

Penelope clung to my arm. "Who are we going to meet exactly?"

"My uncle, aunt, and cousins."

Penelope gazed up at me. "They're in the business, correct?"

"You can say it's something like that."

"Be honest." Penelope tugged on my arm.

"My uncle is a retired don of the Calabresi family; his son Savio took over."

"How many brothers and sisters does Savio have?"

"Four brothers."

"Wow, so you have three siblings, and you lead the Calabresi cartel in New York, and Savio is in Chicago with four brothers. For a total of eight men and 1 girl. I bet your uncle and aunt had a terrible time disciplining you guys."

I chuckled at her statement. "We had no choice but to grow up fast. My parents and uncle weren't hard on us, but we knew what respect meant."

Little Dove nodded.

"Are we going to have the conversation about Tinsley?" Penelope laid her head on my shoulder.

"She worked for me."

Penelope swiftly sat up straight. "That you screwed over and over."

"A few times, but it was always business. I apologize for not seeing it earlier."

"What did Elio say when you told him about killing Tinsley?

I drifted my eyes to her thighs, planting my arm around the back of the seat. "He understood... family over everything."

"Her perfume is what returned me to that night; I remembered smelling that scent in the lobby."

I stretched my hand out to cup her chin and brushed my lips against her mouth. "I should have looked into her deeper. I was so focused on Lucinda and the Bulgarians."

Our arrival at the compound was known from the number of cars parked in the driveway along the street.

"Wow, their home is beautiful."

"Come on, let's get the introductions over, so we can get back home."

Penelope sniggered and thrusted her hand out for me to take, accompanying her up the long gravel stones to the stairs of the front entrance. The house manager greeted us, and I shook hands with Cousin Elio and Vinny.

"Where is Renato and Sante?"

"They're in the kitchen arguing about something." Savio grimaced.

Adelina grinned wide; her arms were spread for a hug. "Who is this beautiful young lady?"

I stepped to the side. "Adelina and Elio Calabresi, Sr., my aunt and uncle."

Penelope blew her air kisses. "Nice to meet you both. I hear a lot of great things."

"My nephew is a kind young man," Adelina expressed.

"Giosuè is like one of my boys, hardheaded and stubborn." Uncle Elio smirked, grabbed my hand, and pulled me in a hug.

"How are you doing?"

"Glad to be back to show off my donna."

My aunt and uncle gasped at the same time. Penelope took in their strange looks. They started to speak in Italian franticly, then clapped their hands.

"So happy for you, Giosuè." Adelina whispered, in my ear.

"Giosuè, like our sons, is very mysterious about his love life, but for him to bring you here means you're special," Uncle Elio said.

"Can we go sit first before you scare her off?" I groaned, holding Penelope to my side.

Renato and Sante came around the corner frowning. "What happened to being single forever?" Renato wrapped an arm around my neck, play boxing.

I pushed him away and waved him off, taking a seat next to Penelope on the couch.

"Where's your son?" I asked.

Renato took a seat on the edge of the couch. "In the backyard with my wife."

"Sante is the second oldest, then Renato." I introduced them to Penelope.

"She's going to love the girls," Sante explained.

"Girls?" Penelope quipped.

"Their wives."

"Rena, come here and meet a better-looking woman than you—besides my wife," Renato joked. All his brothers groaned in unison. Armani and Bosco burst into laughter; I already knew how the two of them got when they were together.

"Renato, if anyone is more attractive in this family, it's my dog." Rena smacked him on the side of the head.

"See, Pops. I told you she's violent," Renato argued.

"Hi, I am Rena, married to Sante." Rena stood next to Sante near the loveseat.

Penelope shook her hand, stretching out her arms for a hug. "Hi, I'm Penelope. I'm glad to meet you and your husband."

"Are you from here?" Rena checked.

Penelope slid back next to me. "New York."

"Any crazy family or psycho exes?" Rena interrogated.

Penelope tittered at her question.

"Rena," I groaned.

"What? I have to make sure the girls are covered. In this family, anything can happen at the drop of a hat," Rena fussed.

"True." Renato motioned at me.

"See if jackass agrees with me..." Rena pouted. Sante roped a hand around her waist.

"Girls come with me outside. The rest of the women are there." Adelina encouraged and linked arms with Rena and Penelope.

Uncle Elio whistled. "She's beautiful, nephew."

"Exactly, so why is she with him?" Renato joked.

I pretended to punch him in the stomach. "Fuck you."

"Bosco, when are you next?" Sante challenged.

"Never." Bosco sucked down the rest of his drink.

Elio Sr. motioned for us to follow him out of the living room, then down the hall to his office.

"Catch me up. Savio and Elio Jr. told me a little bit." He lifted his cigar box, then offered me and the rest of the boys one.

"Time to relax now. You can breathe a little easier. Anything connecting us to the explosion or Lucinda is gone," Savio announced and flicked the light to his cigar.

I blew out the smoke on mine, nodding with my eyes closed for a second.

"I got on Savio for not telling me sooner, but you know better than to keep secrets from me, Giosuè."

I stared back at my uncle's sturdy gaze. "Out of respect, Don, I wanted to make it without any interference from the family."

"Family is supposed to protect each other. You are my blood."

"I know."

"Then don't let it happen again. And I hear the girl graduated from law school and works at Elio's firm?"

"She does."

"For him to almost start a war means she's extra special." Renato clapped me on the shoulder.

"I hope to have more grandkids running around here."

"Not from me." Renato jumped up and stalked out of the office.

"He's an idiot," Elio hissed.

"Your brother," I joked.

"So, Bosco, tell us your grievances." Uncle Elio pointed at my brother.

Bosco plopped down on the chair, crossed a leg at the ankle, and clasped his fingers together.

"I received a message today pertaining to me having to travel back to Italy."

"For what?"

Bosco raised up in the seat, removed his phone, and placed it on top of my uncle's desk.

"Something going on with the Graziano family."

"When did you get this email?" Don Elio Sr. wondered.

"After I got a call from one of your top men in Italy," Bosco responded.

"Make sure you keep us updated if Savio needs to go with you," Don Elio Sr. stated.

"No problems will come to your doorstep, Uncle," I promised.

He rose from the chair and came around to sit on the edge. "You boys have grown into men-- loyal, trustworthy, and spirited. A little too spirited at times."

Everybody burst out laughing.

"Come on. We go eat and enjoy the children." Don Elio Sr. led us to the backyard, where there was a pool full of kids, swimming and playing. Penelope's head fell back in laughter at something Nyla said. Each cousin had the love of their woman to keep them moving forward, and I now had the same thing that kept me grounded and nourished enough to stay wise.

Renato Jr. and Savio Jr. pretended to play cops and robbers. They ran right up to me, and I squatted in front of them and pretended to let them arrest me by holding up the toy gun. "What are arresting me for?"

Savio Jr. giggled. "Our money."

"Yeah!" Renato Jr. jumped up and down.

"How much do I owe you?"

Savio paused for a minute. "One dollar." He held up a finger.

"Boys, stop asking for money." Mckayla strolled over, snatched the money out of their hands, and gave it back to me.

"Giosuè, stop spoiling them—and Savio, I told you about buying them guns." Mckayla huffed, snatching the toys from them.

Savio narrowed his eyes at his wife's ass while she sauntered back to the women in the corner sitting on cabana chairs.

"Better listen to your donna," I jested.

"Shut up." Savio slapped me on the back of the head.

We had laughs, conversations, and great food every day for a week. Spending time with my little cousins and learning their personalities above all reminded me of their fathers when they were younger.

Chapter 19

Penelope

Giosuè and I had just come back from the trip to Chicago. Meeting his family had meant so much to me. Then he had to fly out to do business in California, which felt like a long year instead of a week. I let most of the staff have today off and finished baking the potatoes and onions. Cooking for my boyfriend wasn't new to me, but Giosuè always gave me a hard time about me not allowing people to do things for us. I turned the knob up on the radio, snapping my fingers and letting my shoulders roll. Life was immensely better and calmer since Lucinda and Tinsley were out of my life. Maggie was the only one left. I encouraged her to go out for a spa day with friends, but she insisted on staying in case we needed help. I made it my goal to treat him to dinner and relaxation for the rest of the day with a movie and cuddling. I grabbed the bottle of white wine and poured what was left of the contents in my glass, then closed my eyes, taking another sip.

"Mmmmmm."

I smelled him before he touched me around my waist with his hands traveling down my thigh.

"Welcome home."

The scent of his dark musky cologne seeped into the air as he kissed the back of my head and the side of my neck.

"I missed you."

Twisting around in front of him, expanded my arms around his neck, smoothly cupped the back of his head. "I missed you more."

"Show me." There was a gleam of interest in his blue eyes, and he pushed his hips against mine. I moaned, ready to feel him again. Not having him close for a week was hard; I felt like my heart was in two different places.

I raised my left leg over his waist, kissing him on the lips lightly. "First night I slept alone, I thought about you when I pleased myself."

"I told you to never touch yourself without me." His eyes gazed down my legs, up to my mouth.

The prolonged anticipation of his hands roaming across my body left me on fire. Giosuè put me on top of the counter next to the stove and turned it off.

"We should eat first; I know you're tired and hungry."

"Only thing I want is your sweet, gentle lips sucking every drop from my dick."

I urgently took off his clothes, while he yanked my shorts down and ripped the shirt that I was wearing. It was the one of his that I often wore when he left. I dreamed of being crushed within his embrace. I felt a tingling in the pit of my stomach at the first touch of his hands raking along the sides of my breasts. We felt like teenagers who couldn't stay away from each other for long after the initial pleasing intimacy struck.

"Baby," I cooed. My mouth opened as his tongue pressed on my bud. Suddenly breathless, I was freed from all the hurt and pain; only Giosuè was locked in my thoughts.

He dipped his head lower, licked the inside of my thigh, lingering kisses and small bites that left me on a high.

My teeth sunk into my bottom lip. I felt lightheaded from his hands sliding up my stomach, then around my waist.

I ran a hand over my breasts, twisted my nipple. "Keep going."

"Thought you were hungry." He chuckled, making me blush. He lifted me off the counter and pulled me his chest, sucking on my tongue. I draped my arm around his shoulder feeling his dick poke at my entrance.

We both gasped at the connection. "Feels like the first time," Giosuè groaned, sweetly burying his head in my neck.

"Ohhh, yes."

"Little Dove taking me so good."

"Yes, please don't stop." My chest melted against him; I wanted to be in his skin. Our breaths quickened, our pace picked up, and I clutched his shoulders to keep our balance.

"Fuck!"

The pressure was too much; my head was spinning, and my fingers ran up to his throat. I squeezed a little, making his eyes darken. Giosuè removed us from the wall and gently put me on the top of the island. I giggled at his attempts at trying to hold it together.

Slap!

Giosuè smacked me on the ass, tugged me back to his waist, and thrusted forward, almost making us fall to the ground.

"Giosuè, please." I saw my heart reflected in his gaze.

"I fucking missed your pussy, and you're here, touching yourself?"

"I'm sorry. Baby." My heart pounded at his movements.

He accepted all my faults. "How sorry?" A quiet passion, maybe a match that wasn't perfect, but it was damn close.

"I will do anything."

He leaned forward and inhaled the scent of my hair. "You will take the punishment of only two orgasms."

"Yes, sir."

He warm body enveloped me.

"You were a bad girl." He exhibited a raw sensuality.

I rocked into him, slid my hand between my legs, brushed a hand over his balls. "Very bad."

Slap!

"Little Dove, you're dangerous."

I arched down lower to meet his thrusts. "Fuck, I'm about to come."

Giosuè bent forward, pressing in harder and faster, clinging to me like I was his last breath. "Come for me, Penelope," he whispered in a raspy voice.

"Giosuè," I cried out his name and convulsed around his thick shaft, leaving me weak and wanting more. He lifted his hips, driving himself even deeper. Shivering at the husky tone of his voice, I couldn't resist his potent brand of sensuality.

"God damn. Shit, Penelope." I leaned forward, then turned to take him in my mouth, never feeling such an exhilarating response to any man. To have the connection come through his moans and grunts had the aura of a feeling no other woman left on his soul. The reality of the life we'd built had come true, and I wanted to keep us longing for each other forever. As I pulled back, I popped him out of my throat. I stroked him up and down, spit on the tip again, and rubbed it on my bottom lip.

"I want my come all over your face, Little Dove."

It was a definite turn-on to be covered in his seed. I took the head down as far as I could go and moved up and down, faster and faster.

"Here it comes."

I loved the curve of his mouth, the side that other people didn't see, the gentleness in his eyes when he looked at me and the graceful strength of his hands when he held me.

"Mmmmm..."

"Shit. Move, baby."

"Come on me now." I sat up with my breasts pushed together and my mouth open, watching him stroke his dick and spread his cum.

"Ugh... catch it all," he grunted.

I watched his body stiffen, releasing all over me. I swiped some cum off my chest and sucked it on my tongue. Then my fingers moved down to my lower lips. I didn't let the intense stare-off distract me.

"You're my dirty little whore."

"Yes, sir."

* * *

The smooth sound of ocean waves floated in the air, as I laid flat on the massage table, feeling every knot being poked and prodded. Giosuè had planned for me and the girls to spend the day at the spa again, while he worked at the office. It was Saturday, and the law firm was closed so Elio could have a meeting with the top partners and assistants. The situation with Tinsley put a dark cloud on the team, and Agnes was upset because she'd introduced me to Tinsley and had no clue about her relationship with Giosuè.

"My entire body really needed a day to myself," Rena explained.

"Me too. Before I get back to work, I want to be rejuvenated."

Mckayla and Nyla walked over wearing their robes and holding glasses of mimosas. "Are we ready for our facials?"

"Facials and drinking is my type of party." Aspen grinned.

"So, all you guys are married, right?" Lucy stood, captured her robe, and followed us to the next room.

"I'm married to Savio the oldest, and Rena is married to Sante, and Nyla got stuck with the baby brother, Vinny," Mckayla answered.

"My man has nothing baby on him." Nyla snapped her fingers, and Rena high-fived her.

The entire afternoon floated by with great food, laughs, and conversation. The ladies had come in yesterday to spend some time with me, while their husbands remained in Chicago, watching the kids. At first, Giosuè had been annoyed because we'd stayed up most of the night, and me getting into bed around three in the morning had messed with his sleep pattern.

"I love that color blue on you."

Rena pretended to pose like a model on a runway.

Once the spa was done, Macsen drove our group to the mall and we had the Carolina Herrera store locked down for us to shop alone.

"I could wear it on a date with my husband." Rena removed the hanger on another dress to go change.

"Aspen and Lucy okay with your lifestyle now?" Mckayla investigated.

"They seem to be fine. At first, it was scary—even for me—but Giosuè has calmed down a little with his stalking." I sniggered at my joke.

"We all have those men who took it upon themselves to be possessive and arrogant." Nyla sighed.

"Savio always reminds me about meeting him at a club." Mckayla giggled.

"No one has a better story than Renato and Angel," Rena jested, putting the white dress back on the rack.

"Leave my husband out of any stories of how we met. I still get nightmares." Angel shuddered and laughed at her own joke. She'd filled me in on how she'd met her future husband one night working as a stripper. They had a one-night stand, and she left him the next morning alone in bed. A year later Renato learned she'd had a baby he knew nothing about.

"We have come a long way, and now we get to have a new sister join the fun," Mckayla teased, pinching my cheek.

"Come on, let's try on more dresses. I want to surprise Giosuè with a date," I suggested.

"Remember, surprise him with a little leg or titty action; that always works for Sante after an argument," Rena joked.

"Ignore Rena. I like the yellow jumper you picked up." Mckayla pointed at the clothes I had on my arm.

"Before I return to work, I want to spend as much time as possible with him."

"Are you planning on having kids?"

"Not right now. We never really talked about kids."

"You have plenty of time before you make a decision on kids," Mckayla remarked.

"She's right. For now, find something sexy and go take care of you man." Aspen pushed me into the dressing room.

The girls all left to go back to the hotel. Aspen and Lucy drove home. I piled my bags near the door and thanked Macsen for dealing with all those different personalities. I followed the low sound of a television playing and shuffled into the living room. I spotted Giosuè laid out with a boxing match on the TV screen. I gently touched his hand to take the remote and switch the television off. He gripped my hand and twisted my body around to lie flat on top of him.

"Giosuè!"

He grinned and smashed a kiss on my forehead. "Sneaking in here to turn the TV off?"

"I was trying to be polite, since you weren't watching it. A movie was playing that I wanted to watch."

"A movie?"

I pecked him on the lips. "Yeah."

Giosuè snuggled my body against his chest. "What's the movie?"

"*Romeo and Juliet.*" It felt like things came easy for us now that all the secrets were out in the open. Every day, it was a blessing to wake up and find out something new about him.

He rolled his eyes, and I laughed at the grimace on his face.

"Any movie in the world and you want to watch *Romeo and Juliet.*"

"A tragic love story."

"I got your tragic love story right here." He smacked me on the ass.

I played with his bottom lip. "Ouch! Our story wasn't tragic, just a little chaotic."

Giosuè grabbed my hand. "Chaotic is the best word you could use."

"Come on, let's watch it together."

"I have work to do."

"I thought you worked earlier at the office."

"I have files to read over." He started to climb from under me and I eased my hand on top of his dick and squeezed.

"Are you sure that can't wait?" I was mad with lust, hungry for another round in his playroom.

He groaned. "You love playing with fire."

"I can stop." I yanked my hand away.

Giosuè cupped my chin and slipped his tongue into my mouth. "Why watch the movie when we can make our own?" Giosuè arched his left brow.

"First one to the playroom gets to call the shots!" I jumped up to start running, and he grasped me around the waist, bridal style, making us both laugh.

He squeezed me around the waist. "I call the shots—in *or* out of the playroom."

"Little Dove has been a bad girl lately." I moaned.

He was all man, hot and hard.

"You ready for your punishment?"

"Make it hurt, sir." I didn't need gentle this time.

He marched out of the house, then around the backyard to the side room. He put the key in the door, placed me on my feet, and shut it behind him.

"Get on your knees, Little Dove."

I was wild, open and willing.

Epilogue: Giosuè

I ambled through the entrance to my office, peeked into the kitchen, and picked up a glass of juice. My day had been long, and I had plans to spend it with my girls, but work needed to get handled first thing in the morning. Penelope had the time of her life sightseeing around Italy with her friends. I glanced at Maggie coming to the door and waved inside.

"What are you doing here so early?"

"I got the call about the meeting."

"What meeting?" Guilianna sprinted into the kitchen, wearing a sports bra and shorts after her run.

"Where have you been?"

Guilianna jumped up and down, then stretched her legs and arms. "Penelope wanted to go workout, but she went with her friends, but I decided to still go."

Maggie passed Guilianna a bottle of water.

"I will have brunch ready for you soon," Maggie said.

I shoved my sleeve back to check the time. "Penelope should be on the way back now."

Guilianna rested on the island. "Tell me about this meeting."

"Right now, it's under control, but we have to inform Uncle soon," Bosco remarked.

"Handle it. This is my vacation."

Bosco and Guilianna grinned at me.

"Big Brother is actually taking time for himself?" Guilianna teased, jumping down from the kitchen island and tossing the empty bottle into the trash.

"Shut up, G."

Guilianna laughed at me.

"Aspen that was so fun." Penelope strolled into the kitchen, holding hands with Aspen and Lucy. She released her arm and pushed her bags on top of the table, then jogged to jump in my arms, smashing her lips on mine.

"I missed you."

"I missed you more, Little Dove." I sucked on her tongue.

"Get a room you two." Guilianna pretended to gag.

Penelope pulled back and stood on her feet. "Sorry, G. How was the run?"

"It could have been great if you would have come with me," Guilianna grumbled.

"Sorry, friend, next time if your brother doesn't keep me up all night," Penelope confessed.

Guilianna and Bosco shook their heads in disgust.

"She's my girlfriend."

"Anyway, Penelope, how is the job going?" Guilianna asked.

"Fine. I have a week before I need to head back and Elio has some plans for me to start really meeting with family lawyers to get some experience," Penelope explained.

Guilianna picked up a napkin to wipe her face. "So happy to hear about you working more on cases now."

"Just spending my parents' money." Lucy shrugged.

"Babe, come with me." I stuck my hand out, and Penelope followed me from the kitchen.

"Where are we going?"

"I want to take you on a drive."

"Where? I'm not really dressed."

I picked her up and threw her over my shoulder. "You trust me?"

"Yes."

I smacked her on the ass again. "Then let me run the show."

Penelope had no clue that my parents were born close to our home, and I wanted to take her to a place that meant the most to me and let her see where our legacy started. Macsen stayed back, and I hopped on my motorcycle, handed Penelope a helmet for her protection, and sped away from our mansion. My father had a private burial ground built many years ago that held all our relatives; it was where I wanted to be buried when it was my time.

We arrived a minute later. I let her step off first, slid my helmet from my head, and took hers off too.

"A burial ground." Penelope stepped back in confusion.

"My family's plot." The green pastures were surrounded by masses of flowers, with each family member having a tombstone with their picture. There was a large sign of our family name on the iron gates. Security walked through every few hours to make sure nothing was out of place.

"Why are we here?"

"I want to introduce you."

Tears started to well up in her eyes.

"Giosuè."

"Come on. I want the most important person in my life to meet the other most important people I love."

Penelope swung my head around to place a kiss on my lips.

"Penelope, this is my father and mother, Mr. Giosuè and Mrs. Liliana Calabresi." I dusted off the leaves and dirt from the tombstone plaque.

It held both of their pictures and dates.

"Penelope's someone special. I can admit I got her under different circumstances, but she's all mine."

Penelope grinned.

"Thank you, Giosuè."

"Thank you for being here." I dropped to my knees and removed a black box from my coat pocket.

Penelope wiped the tears from her eyes and fanned herself.

"Penelope, in front of my parents and the people I love, will you marry me?"

"Give him an answer!" Bosco shouted.

Penelope stumbled in surprise and laughed at everyone being there. I'd wanted the moment to be intimate, but I felt that my brothers, my sister, and Penelope's friends would want to be a part of our special occasion too.

"You planned this by yourself?" Penelope got down on her knees.

"Is there going to be an answer from you?"

She threw her arms around my neck. "Yes. I love you, Giosuè!"

I cupped the back of her head and kissed her cheek, sliding the ring on her finger.

"To death do us part."

"I think we'll end up like your parents—buried together. I mean, you did stalk me for a reason."

* * *

I hope you enjoyed Penelope and Giosue's story. Please also check out the sneak peek of Bosco's story here.

Start from the beginning with **Savio: Age Gap, Forced Proximity Forced Marriage Book 1** https://books2read.com/u/mlEAW7

Follow it up with a Dark Mafia Enemies to Lovers Arranged Marriage "**Sante: Dark Mafia Billionaire Romance:** Book 2 https://books2read.com/u/mdd1oW

Also, if you love Hate To Love, Marriage of Convenience "**Renato: Dark Mafia Billionaire Romance:** Book 3 https://books2read.com/u/4AjAQd

Plus, a Second chance, Dark Mafia Romance "**Elio: Dark Mafia Billionaire Romance**: Book 4 https://books2read.com/u/4j5yjD

Fans of Debt romance will continue to love. "**Vincenzo: A Debt Owed, Enemies to Lovers Dark Mafia Billionaire Romance**:Book 5 https://books2read.com/u/4EEYYo

Sneak Peek: Bosco

Giselle never imagined herself becoming a young widow, or falling in love with a billionaire....

Giselle was fighting for her life when she first caught Bosco's eye. That very same night, she lost her husband and her world came crashing down. When Bosco steps back into her life, she doesn't recognize him from that fateful night, and finds the billionaire not only handsome, but there for her in a time of need.

Regardless of their age difference, Giselle allows Bosco into her heart. She knows he has secrets, but who doesn't. Only, she doesn't realize the biggest secret Bosco has, is the one that cost her husband his life, and threatened hers.

When she discovers his cartel ties, Giselle tries to pull away, but she's already in too deep. Will she submit to Bosco's desire for her, or will she be claimed instead?

If you enjoy steamy romances, billionaires rescuing damsels in distress, and age gap affairs, then you'll love Bosco.

Sneak Peek: Armani

A one-night stand with a mafia billionaire turns deadly when Kristina learns it's her father's greatest rival.

Kristina was ready to escape her family and the family business. When she succumbs to a night of passion with a handsome stranger, she never imagined the trail of events that would follow. Especially when she learns that their families are rivals and Armani begins to blackmail her to hurt her family.

Armani Calabresi is determined to get revenge for his father's death. As the youngest of three brothers, he brings to light a longstanding feud between rivaling families that many would've rather kept under wraps. He knew that sleeping with Kristina would hit her father where it would hurt the most. He just didn't expect to *want* to sleep with her again.

They might have mistaken each other for lovers, but now it's clear they're enemies. Whose family will win the war? Or will they destroy each other instead?

Acknowledgments

I want to dedicate this to my team that helps me behind the scenes, from my editors, test readers, graphic designers, and the list goes on. I truly appreciate each of you for keeping me on my toes.

Calabresi Mafia Series

Savio: Book 1

https://books2read.com/u/mlEAW7

Sante: Book 2

https://books2read.com/u/mdd1oW

Renato: Book 3

https://books2read.com/u/4AjAQd

Elio : Book 4

https://books2read.com/u/4j5yjD

Vincenzo: Book 5

https://books2read.com/u/4EEYYo

Thank you so much for reading. If you enjoyed the crazy ride and decide to leave a review, we'd appreciate the support.

About the Author

L.K. Ryan is an author of Romantic Suspense, Dark Romance, and Contemporary Novels. Join my newsletter and sign up for the latest news and updates on my books and releases: